There was

'Aidan. . .' sh

Panic rose in sick, get off at Lisbon, then first port of call, fly home as soon as they sent out a replacement. But Shelly knew she would not do that. She liked her job too much to let everyone down. She had let Aidan ruin her career prospects at Kingham's. She was not about to let him do the same on the *Clipper Countess*.

Stella Whitelaw's writing career began as a cub reporter on a local newspaper. She became one of the first and youngest women chief reporters in London. While bringing up her small children she had many short stories published in magazines. She is deeply interested in alternative medicines, and is glad that her son, now a doctor and anaesthetist, has an open mind about them. A painful slipped disc has improved since practising the Alexander Technique daily.

Recent titles by the same author:

DELUGE
A CERTAIN HUNGER

CRUISE DOCTOR

BY
STELLA WHITELAW

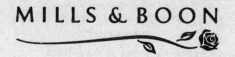

MILLS & BOON

To
Dr Sally Bell and her medical team

*MILLS & BOON, the Rose Device and
LOVE ON CALL are trademarks of the publisher.
Harlequin Mills & Boon Limited,
Eton House, 18-24 Paradise Road, Richmond, Surrey TW9 1SR*

© Stella Whitelaw 1996

ISBN 0 263 79468 7

*Set in Times 11 on 12½ pt. by
Rowland Phototypesetting Limited
Bury St Edmunds, Suffolk*

03-9602-40047

*Made and printed in Great Britain
Cover illustration by Simon Bishop*

CHAPTER ONE

'I HAD a dream, a dream of a lady in white,' he said. 'A woman I could cherish and care for, love from afar, spend my life travelling the world with her, taking her to foreign shores to show off her beauty. This was my dream from boyhood. To command a ship with the raking lines of a clipper, that clean, sweeping line to the bow that catches my breath every time I look at her.'

Dr Shelly Smith was momentarily shocked. She had not expected their brusque, ex-Royal Navy captain to have such a sentimental heart. The crew and passengers only saw the unemotional, efficient officer on the bridge, and here was Captain Bellingham going on about dreams and raking lines of beauty. . . The audience was silent with delight.

Shelly had not heard the captain's lecture before. She had slipped into the back of the theatre, seeking darkness for a pounding head-ache, not really watching the slides. She had been worked off her feet all morning with sea-sick passengers and cabin calls. The Bay of Biscay was taking its toll and the ten o'clock surgery had been full of unhappy patients only too willing to bare their pale-skinned rumps for a stabilising injection. The men were the worst.

'Gently, now, Doctor. I can't stand needles!'

The *Clipper Countess* was beautiful, starkly white and remote with the sweeping line of an ocean clipper. Shelly, too, felt a thrill every time she saw the liner in dock or at anchor off shore, sought her shape for reassurance as if looking for a lost lover in a crowd.

A lost lover in a crowd. She was always seeing him, or thinking that she saw him. His height, the familiar stoop as he peered to see closer, the achingly sharp profile of his face and dark head, the glint of steel-rimmed glasses. It was all she could do to stop herself rushing up to every dark-haired man over six feet two.

'Shelly Smith,' she said to herself in the cool gloom of the theatre. 'Stop being a fool and grow up. You've had enough time to get over him.' But her nails bit into the palms of her hands as she clenched them.

Even after three years, Shelly felt a stab of loss remembering the heady happiness of her very first serious love affair. She had been newly qualified, a junior doctor at the illustrious Kingham General Hospital, eager to learn and absorb wisdom from her masters. She had worked all hours of the day and night without complaint, staggering back to her room like a zombie after a long, tiring shift. In the early hours of a December morning Shelly had staggered right into the arms of Aidan Trent.

'Why, here's an early bird who's up before the

dawn chorus,' he'd said gently, steadying her on her feet. 'Looking for your nest?'

She had wondered if the rugged, almost good-looking Aidan Trent had been returning from a late party. Everyone at Kingham's knew about the senior consultant's mad social whirl. He'd looked tousled and tired but still with a twinkle in those clear and vibrant grey eyes.

'So, you're one of our new intake of baby doctors,' Aidan continued, steering her towards her room. 'I thought I'd seen you hovering on the edge of ward rounds, listening to my every word.'

He was not being pompous. There was a gleam of self-mockery in his eyes and in the timbre of his deep voice. Then Shelly remembered rumours of rushed emergency surgery upstairs that night and a five-hour-long bypass operation. Suddenly he stroked the long fall of her fine, silky hair round her face as if looking for some kind of comfort. She saw the tiredness etched in the broad slope of his shoulders and fell in love with him as fast as that. It happened instantly. She loved him without question. There was nothing she would not do for him.

Shelly shook herself out of her daydream. She thought she had cured herself of thinking about him, of wasting her life with useless hopes. She could not allow herself to be seduced by a memory. Three years working on the *Clipper Countess* was a long time and a million watery miles between them had brought her back to her senses.

She looked at her watch and straightened the slim white skirt and immaculately pressed shirt that were her working uniform. Only the red shoulder tabs denoted her medical status. Her long brown hair was twisted up now into a neat, elegant chignon, her skin was always a honey-tan, and her make-up only discreet eye-liner and mascara.

The medical centre was down on Deck E, sign-posted through the labyrinth of corridors, past the beauty parlour and barber's shop. She wondered how her patients ever found it. But once they were seated in the comfortable waiting-room, everything familiar and medically normal around them, her own brand of caring attention was ready to put them at ease. Being sick on a long voyage could be frightening, so far from home, so far from their local GP. It was her responsibility to reassure as well as cure.

'Good afternoon,' she said, smiling as she went through the crowded waiting area to her consulting-room. 'I won't keep you waiting long. Please give to Sister your name, cabin number and the reason you are here. Sister Frances will be able to do any treatments straight away.'

Shelly had two sisters on her staff; Frances was also a midwife and Jane was a physiotherapist and X-ray technician. She had a personal Goanese steward, Dino, and special crew for the running of the three two-bedded wards for passengers and the crew ward. There was also an emergency-room fully equipped for intensive care with defibrillator, ventilator and heart-monitoring equipment. A last small cabin was an isolation unit which Shelly always hoped she would not have to use. Offices, dispensary, sluice and wash-rooms made up the rest of her small, compact empire.

She washed her hands and went to welcome her first patient. It was an elderly gentleman using a walking stick. He looked too frail to be taking a month-long cruise. Shelly often thought some of her patients would be safer on dry land at Eastbourne. But they were hooked on cruising and determined to get about at all costs. There were three wheelchair passengers on this voyage, all of whom needed a daily visit from her.

One of the wheelchair passengers was ter-minally ill with cancer but she knew the family wanted to cope on their own. She had seen him already, and although he had a sweet smile his eyes raged with the unfairness of it all. He was still a young man, in his late thirties.

'We can manage,' his wife had insisted. 'Our two sons help with the lifting. We want this cruise to be as normal as possible. A real family holiday.'

Shelly had to admire and respect their wishes. But now she put this sad case out of mind and turned her attention to the first patient.

'Mr Howard. How nice to see you again. Last

year on the Canaries cruise, wasn't it? And how is your arthritis these days?'

As she spoke she took Cyril Howard's notes out of her files. They were sent to her from the Southampton office each cruise, giving her all known medical details of passengers.

'Are you still on the same medication?' she asked.

'Yes, Dr Smith,' he said, gripping hard on his stick as he sat down. 'But, like a fool, I've left all my pills at home. I wouldn't bother you but I can't get about without them. Mind you, this little bit of rough sea doesn't bother me. I've still got my sea legs if nothing else.'

'No problem,' said Shelly. 'I'll prescribe a week's supply of your medication, then perhaps you'd come back to me when you've finished them. I'd like to keep an eye on you, just to make sure everything is all right.'

'You're very kind, Doctor. I remember how good you were with my Ethel when she had that upset tummy.'

Shelly heard the heartbreak in his voice and knew immediately without asking. He was on his own now.

'Your wife? She's not with you?'

He shook his head sadly. 'No, she passed away last winter. Pneumonia, y'know. We had planned this cruise as a special one. Golden wedding anniversary. I didn't want to come without her but everyone said it would do me good.'

'I'm sure Ethel would have wanted you to take the trip. And it will do you good. Weren't you the star of the super quiz game every evening last year?'

He brightened and chuckled. 'I've lived so long I can remember practically everything. No other team stands a chance.'

'Go ahead and win again. Ethel would be pleased.'

'I might just do that.'

Shelly made a mental note of his cabin number. She worried about new widowers. They seemed to have less will to live whereas the spritely widows were out there learning the samba and making new friends.

She was in the middle of listening to the complaints of a diabetic who insisted that the kitchens were not getting his diet right, when her bleeper went off. The call was from Deck A, one of the luxury stateroom suites. She sighed, pushing back straying wisps of hair. Luxury staterooms often meant trouble.

'Don't worry, Mr Armstrong. I'll have a word with the chef de cuisine and make sure you get your meals exactly as required. We don't want any problems, and nutrition as well as food selection is important. You're supposed to be enjoying your cruise. Check your urine sample every morning and remember your insulin and you'll be fine. It's controllable these days. Now, if you'll excuse me. I have a cabin call.'

'Thank you, Doctor. I knew you'd put things right.'

She scribbled a note and gave it to Frances as she hurried out with her medical case. 'Check Mr Armstrong's diet with the chef when you get a moment, Frances. The wires have got crossed somewhere along the line.'

She ran up the stairs, not waiting for the lift. No wonder she was so slim, all the stairs she did in a day. All the lifts would be busy with passengers going to their cabins to get ready for the captain's cocktail party before the first sitting for dinner in the Collingwood Restaurant. All officers had to host a dinner table, and because of evening surgery she hosted an eight-seater table at the second sitting. But her chair was often vacant. Passengers allocated to her table drew a short straw.

She slowed down as she got to the wider corridor where the best outside cabins were situated. It wouldn't do for any top-paying passenger to see the ship's doctor running.

She stopped suddenly, letting some passengers pass her, hardly aware of their passing, smiling pleasantly. Her heart was pounding in an alarming manner and it was not just the stairs. She could not believe what she was seeing. . .

Across the mirrored landing, a tall man was peering closely at the brass inscription under a maritime oil painting. The shape of his dark head caught sharply at her heart-strings; the glint of glasses were reflected in the mirrors. Every strand of well-cut dark hair was familiar, brought a tingling to her veins as she remembered the feel of tangling her fingers in its thickness.

'Aidan. . .' she breathed. There was no mistake.

The man straightened up and her mouth went dry. No two men could wear such an aura of authority, of isolation, of mysterious secrecy. It was Aidan Trent. The man she never wanted to see again, vowed never to see again. And he was on the *Clipper Countess* as a passenger, it seemed.

She closed her eyes for an instant, shutting out the image of his stooped figure. But it was still there, imprinted on her retina. There were seven hundred passengers on the cruise. If she kept her head down she needed not meet him. She knew every inch of the ship, needed never mix with the customers. Yet the hopelessness of such a plan did not escape her. A month of hiding in the medical centre was impossible, and she was expected to do her share of circulating at social functions. She got cabin calls day and night. She could hardly hibernate.

Panic rose in waves. Perhaps she should go sick, get off at Lisbon, their first port of call, fly home as soon as they sent out a replacement. But Shelly knew she would not do that. She liked her job too much to let everyone down. She had let Aidan ruin her career prospects at Kingham's. She was not about to let him do the same on the *Clipper Countess*.

She paused outside the door of the stateroom suite, trying to remember who she had come to see.

She knocked smartly. 'Ah, Mrs Scott-Card. I'm Dr Smith. How can I help you?'

Shelly recognised Mrs Avril Scott-Card immediately. The lifeboat drill muster before leaving Southampton had been enlivened by Mrs Scott-Card's refusal to put on the bulky life-jacket. She had flatly refused, protesting that she had just had her hair done.

'I'm not putting that stupid thing over my head and ruining my hairdo,' she had said repeatedly, patting her sleek platinum crop. 'I paid good money for this. What a waste of time. Cruise liners are supposed to be safe. I'm going back to my cabin.'

'It's in your own interests to know what to do in an emergency,' one of the officers had said patiently.

'I shall expect you to come and rescue me,' Mrs Scott-Card had replied, parting her glossy lips in a smile. Even her lipstick spelled money. 'That's what you're paid for.'

The officer had wilted under the smile but had not dropped his well-trained politeness. 'Of course,' he had said. 'We'll take good care of you.'

He had turned away and winked at Shelly. 'You'll get a medal for bravery,' she had said in an aside as she had gone to help anyone in a twist with tying their life-jacket strings.

Avril Scott-Card was now draped along the comfortable sofa that flanked the two big picture windows of the day area of their suite. She was wearing tight gold lamé trousers and a skimpy shirt knotted under her bosom. She was already tanned a golden bronze from hours under a sunbed.

'You've taken your time, Doctor,' she said. 'I called ages ago.'

'I came straight away even though I had to leave evening surgery,' said Shelly evenly. She moved over to the woman, noting the ashtray full of stubs and generous glass of gin on the table. 'Would you like to tell me what's the matter?'

'I'm feeling really awful,' said Mrs Scott-Card, closing her eyes. 'My stomach. It hurts.'

'Any nausea? Pain?' Shelly noted that her patient did not actually look ill, or flinch as Shelly examined her. Minor abdominal pain was the hardest ailment to diagnose. It could be a simple case of indigestion or the effects of overeating or alcohol. But it could be an abdominal emergency such as appendicitis or a perforated or duodenal ulcer, which would mean surgical treatment ashore. Shelly could cope with minor operations but anything major was beyond her at present.

Then she thought of Aidan Trent. He was on board. He was one of the top consultant surgeons in London. But to ask for his help would be a

blow to her pride and a very last resort. It was
going to be difficult enough just seeing Aidan on
board ship—she would find it hard to hide her
true feelings for him.

Shelly checked her patient's blood-pressure,
temperature. All was normal. She palpatated the
abdomen, watching if anything moved with the
woman's breathing.

'Could you cough, please?' said Shelly.
'Where's the pain when you cough?'

Mrs Scott-Card vaguely waved over her
stomach, wriggling on the couch and sighing. 'It's
everywhere.'

Shelly wondered what to do. Mrs Scott-Card
was clearly not in any real pain. Most patients lay
very still and appeared to be afraid to move
or cough on account of the pain. If, for some
personal reason, she wanted and insisted on
being diagnosed with something serious, then
Shelly would be forced to recommend that she
be flown home from Lisbon for further tests.
If she just wanted attention and to become
an interesting invalid then Shelly had to think
quickly.

Shelly took a deep breath. 'For a start, Mrs
Scott-Card, I would suggest that you'd be more
comfortable in clothes that did not fasten so
tightly. Look at the marks on your stomach and
under your breasts. No wonder you're in pain.
That belt is strangling your stomach and small
intestine and the wiring of this uplift bra is lethal

for your breathing. Extreme restriction isn't good for the digestive system.'

'But all my clothes fit tightly. I have an excellent figure and my husband likes me to show it off.'

'Then I suggest your husband takes you shopping in the boutique and buys you some new clothes that allow you to breathe and digest your food. Meanwhile I'll prescribe a mild indigestion compound and suggest you keep to a simple diet for a few days. No fried food, spicy food or alcohol till you feel better.'

'Will I be able to go to the captain's welcome-aboard cocktail party this evening?' Mrs Scott-Card asked anxiously. The idea of buying some new clothes was already working wonders.

'In a couple of hours you'll be feeling fine.' Shelly wrote out a prescription for magnesium trisilicate. 'I'll get this sent up to you right away, and I look forward to seeing you at the party in some wonderful, floaty creation.'

'Thank you, Doctor. You've been very kind.' Mrs Scott-Card was already sitting up, tidying her face to go shopping. 'Thank you for coming.'

'Not at all. See you at the party.'

And wait till you get my bill, thought Shelly, closing the door behind her. Cabin calls were not cheap. An expensive way to be told she was wearing a bra several sizes too small.

Shelly was smiling to herself as she made her way back to the medical centre. Evening surgery was over and the waiting-room empty. All officers

were expected to attend the party and circulate
among the captain's guests. She would have time
for a shower and to wash her hair and put on a
fresh uniform.

'Am I too late to see you, Doctor?'

Shelly stopped in her tracks. That voice. She
did not have to turn round to know to whom it
belonged. He was close behind her and she was
only too aware of his commanding height even
without looking at him. Yes, it was too late. Too
late for her to run and hide.

Once she had shared her life with him. It had
been a time of such happiness. Then it had all
gone wrong. She knew she had been partly to
blame, but so had Aidan with his stubborn ideas.

'Hello, Aidan.' She composed her face and put
on a professional smile. 'How can I help you?'
she said. A stillness came over her. She drank in
the sight of him thirstily.

It was the first time she had seen Aidan Trent
for three years and the time was wiped out in an
instant. She sought the details of his face to see
if he had changed; the clear grey eyes were the
same and the bristly eyebrows untamed, though
there were a few deeper lines, perhaps, and a
sprinkling of silver in his unruly dark hair. If he
smiled that crazy, lopsided smile she would be
lost. Where was her famous coolness now? She
was as tongue-tied as any schoolgirl. The corridor
went out of focus, swimming into the distance.
Aidan had meant so much to her.

'So we meet again, Shelly,' he said in a tone that was tinged with bitterness. He was looking at her in a strange, questioning way. 'It's been a long time.'

'You knew it was going to be me?' said Shelly, her grammar going to the wall. She was unable to say anything remotely more intelligent. Had she spent six years at medical university to produce this kind of conversation?

'I spotted your smiling face on the crew photoboard outside the purser's office. And they would only have the very best, wouldn't they? The best in cruising, that's the shipping line's motto, isn't it? So the best doctor.'

'Are you a passenger? I mean, are you here on a cruise. . .?' She stumbled over the words, then moistened her lips and tried to take a hold of herself. This was ridiculous. Where had the cool Dr Smith gone? Over the side apparently.

'I'm a passenger like anyone else. I thought I deserved a holiday,' he said evenly, his keen glance sweeping over her, probing her for clues. 'I gave up looking for you ages ago and I'm not going to bring up the past. The fact that you just disappeared without a word, caused everyone a hell of a lot of worry and concern, simply doesn't matter any more.'

His eyes darkened fast. She saw the surge of anger cross his face and in the hunch of his shoulders. For a moment she was deeply frightened; she knew Aidan was capable of towering passion, an explosion of feeling of both anger and love that shattered common sense.

'Is this a social call or. . .? My treatment nurses have gone now but. . .' Shelly tried to retrieve some semblance of normality, in a state of unhappy confusion at this incredibly unnerving experience.

'I need a fresh dressing,' he said, swallowing hard. He was finding it just as difficult. 'Unfortunately I got it wet in the shower, against all the advice of your delectable blonde sister this morning.'

'Frances,' said Shelly automatically. 'You saw her this morning?'

He nodded. 'This has to be dressed every day.'

Now she saw that his left hand was heavily bandaged, but the bandaging was damp and a bit grey. Suddenly he looked like a small boy who'd fallen out of a tree. She had never known Aidan to be ill or hurt before.

'What on earth have you been doing?' she asked, leading him into the treatment-room, welcoming the familiar home ground. 'You can't go to the captain's party with a dirty bandage. I'll put a fresh one on for you.'

'It's not a pretty sight,' said Aidan, sitting down and putting his bandaged hand on the bed. 'But by now you must be used to everything. It's a burn, superficial second degree. Slight altercation with a barbecue.'

Shelly washed her hands and forearms

thoroughly and put on a face mask, glad that the mask would hide her feelings. She cut gently through the wad of old dressing.

'When did you do this?' she asked, showing no emotion at the sight of his hand. The burns had caused deep reddening, considerable swelling and some weeping of fluid. It was mostly over the insides of his fingers and palm of his hand as if he had grasped at something. Fortunately the fingers were not fused and, although they were considerably swollen, he was able to move them independently.

Surgeon's hands. . . Shelly wondered if the nerve ends would be damaged. It was essential for his work that he have the finest control over his hands. How dreadful if this accident put an end to his career.

'Two weeks ago. It was a party in my sister's garden. Someone threw some methylated spirits on the barbecue to get it going and it flared up out of control.'

'How awful,' said Shelly. She didn't ask how he had got burnt. 'But you were lucky. The damage could have been worse. This looks as if it's healing nicely and your mobility's good. Fingers a bit stiff but you should get away with very little scarring.'

They were acting like polite strangers, not saying what they really wanted to say. Yet once they had been so close.

She cleaned the skin very carefully, cleaning

away from the burns in every direction. She clipped off some dead skin, trying not to cause him any pain. Although she was aware of him as a man, a man she had once loved dearly, at that moment he was simply a human in need of her care.

She covered the burn with a paraffin gauze dressing, overlapping, then put on another layer of sterile gauze, and lastly a layer of sterile cotton wool. It was all held in place with a fresh bandage.

'I think that'll see you to the party,' said Shelly. 'And I'll give you some sterile gloves to put on when you take a shower. Just remember to put them on.'

'Thank you, Shelly. It's kind of you.'

'I am a kind person,' she said hesitantly, peeling off her gloves and aiming them at the bin. He would go now and she would make sure she did not see him again.

'But not that kind,' he said aggressively. 'You left me, remember? Without a word. We'd been together for over two years, nearly three and then you left me. Simply vanished into the night. I nearly went mad with worry.'

'I thought we weren't going to mention the past,' said Shelly, fighting to keep the trembling out of her voice. 'I don't want to talk about it and I don't want to start feeling guilty about something I had to do. It's all over and done with. I have a good job with the shipping line and I'm happy. You're here for a well-deserved holiday and the cruise will do you good. Why don't we forget that we ever once knew each other or meant anything to each other?'

She passed her hands wearily over her eyes. She didn't want all this hassle. She wanted to be free of this tall, dark ghost who haunted her dreams.

'If that's what you want,' he snapped, standing up, all expression wiped from his face. He was his own secret man again, giving nothing away.

'Yes, that's what I want,' said Shelly.

They glared at each other. No one would have thought their nights of wonderful lovemaking had ever happened. They had been perfection together, so warm and loving, their wavelengths merging, becoming as one. They'd had more than two wonderful years, deeply in love. The air was vibrant, pulsing with all that lost passion.

'Surely we can be civilised and effect a truce for a month?' Aidan suggested. 'It's not long. I need this holiday.'

The ship lurched and for once Shelly's balance was at fault. She felt swiftly for the edge of the worktop behind her. But Aidan was beside her, his good arm round her waist, and his closeness sent her senses rocketing. She could smell that wonderful clean musk of his skin, remembered long nights of devouring that warm skin with her kisses.

'It's a quartering sea,' she murmured.

'A quartering sea?' Aidan asked as if he didn't understand.

'A sea coming from a forty-five-degree angle either to port or starboard,' she explained vaguely.

'And the going gets rough?'

'The going gets rough. . .' She closed her eyes, and when she opened them again Aidan had done.

CHAPTER TWO

THE captain's party was in full swing, a room full of chatter and laughter, the blue sea rolling by with deceptive serenity outside the picture windows. Captain Bellingham was a good host, spoke to every guest, posed patiently for each photograph. It was held in the spacious Nelson Lounge, a scene remote from the real world, all the women in beautiful dresses and elegant men in evening suits, only the tilt of the floor reminding guests that they were at sea.

Shelly waited along the line of officers, orange juice in her hand, prepared to do her duty with small talk and pleasantries. She was used to the usual comments about her being too young to be a doctor, and what was a nice girl like her doing here? She always got chatted up by the lonely men.

But this time there was something different about her. Her long brown hair hung down her back, looped away from her face with an intricate gold clasp. This abandon was Aidan's doing. Meeting him again with all those confusing emotions had severed some of her inhibitions. To hell with him, she had thought, brushing out her wet hair in the shower.

But when she saw him across the room, head and shoulders taller than anyone else, devastating in an expensive black evening suit and pleated white silk shirt, her heart constricted. She even saw the silk stripe down the edge of his trousers. Men should not be allowed to wear such outfits, she thought. They should be declared lethal, medically dangerous.

She wondered if she was going to be able to last out this party. Then she saw Aidan making his way over to her. She could not take her eyes off him. He was so splendidly tall and handsome, she was barely able to breathe evenly.

'Hello,' he said, as if nothing had happened. 'Nice party.'

'Hello,' she said, feeling ridiculous.

'Are you off duty yet?' He was looking at her over the rim of his glass. His gaze, keen and sharp, set off painful echoes that shattered her protective shell.

'Not till midnight.' She froze herself back into her shell.

'Then I'll see you in the Ensign bar at one minute past. I'll buy you the cocktail of the day. How about a strawberry daiquiri? Don't worry, Doctor, I don't want to talk about my injury. I just want to dance, one-handed. Good for my circulation.'

He left her side without waiting for a reply. As he moved away she wanted to run after him, to take his arm and hold him close. But of course she couldn't. She had ended all that kind of non-sense three years ago, when she had walked out to do what she'd had to do.

'I'm not coming,' she said defiantly but he gave no sign that he had heard.

She blinked back a shimmer of tears quickly. It was not fair. Aidan should not be here, unsettling her new professional life.

Mrs Scott-Card was coming towards her, resplendent in a loose mauve chiffon dress that must have cost the earth. It was obvious that she was not wearing a bra. Shelly knew that particular snippet of information would circulate fast round the junior crew.

'Mrs Scott-Card. You're obviously feeling better,' Shelly said, finding a shaky smile. 'I'm glad.'

'That medicine was wonderful,' said Mrs Scott-Card. 'I'm feeling on top of the world. And isn't this a lovely dress? Fred bought it for me.'

'Beautiful, and it suits you.'

'Thank you so much, my dear. I hope I don't have to see you again.'

They both laughed. 'I know what you mean,' said Shelly, accepting another juice. Her mouth was so dry. 'You'll be able to do even more shopping in Lisbon and Bordeaux. Both have excellent shops.'

'Tell me more. I'm feeling better by the minute.'

Shelly's table of eight at the second sitting were

a lively group—three married couples and a quiet, shy woman called Elaine travelling on her own. It was difficult to get her to talk but the others made up for her silence and the table was soon buzzing with conversation. The six-course meal was as delicious as always, but Shelly had no appetite and only picked at her food, waving away the menu for desserts and savouries.

'If you'll excuse me,' she said, rising. 'I still have some work to do.'

She was remembering the pain of leaving Aidan, of giving up the job she had loved to get away from him; they could never have gone on working in the same hospital.

Back in the medical centre, Shelly caught up with her paperwork and checked the dispensary stock. She hoped she would not have to reorder before the end of the cruise. Most passengers had found their sea legs by the time they returned through the Bay of Biscay.

Shelly's last patient of the day was an Asian crewman who had slipped whilst hosing down the starboard deck and twisted his ankle. He was convinced it was broken but Shelly was sure there was no real damage.

'Very bad, very bad,' he said, shaking his head in despair.

'We'll X-ray it first thing tomorrow morning,' she said cheerfully. 'All this swelling is nature's protection. You've pulled the ligaments. A nasty sprain, that's all.'

She put on a cold compress and recommended a packet of frozen peas from the kitchens applied to the swelling every three or four hours. She deftly wrapped round a crêpe bandage to support his ankle and sent him hobbling back to his quarters with a note for two days' rest and elevation.

Wearily she locked up and went to her cabin at the far end of the medical centre. It was a well-appointed cabin with pale blue furnishings and a real bed, one of the older cabins whose craftsmanship was reflected in its detail. She stood under the shower again, longing for some sleep. There was no way she was going to meet Aidan in the Ensign bar at this time of night.

The phone rang and she wrapped herself in a towel and went to answer it. Technically Jane was on duty now and all calls would be put through to her. Jane would only call her if there was an emergency.

'I've set up your strawberry daiquiri on the bar,' said Aidan. 'Get dressed and come on up here. The disco is just getting going and I know how you like to dance.'

'I'm in bed,' said Shelly flatly.

'Liar. I can hear the shower running.'

And Shelly could hear the music. He was ringing from the Ensign bar and suddenly she realised how much she missed dancing. She rarely mixed with the passengers unless required to by her social duties. Dancing to the small hours in the disco every night was no way to cope with the pressures of her job.

'I'm sorry, Aidan. . .our truce doesn't include dancing.'

'Shall I come and get you? I will, you know.'

His voice was pure seduction. It evoked such memories of love and laughter. It had been a timeless affair, when they had floated through the days, each counting the seconds till they saw each other, their minds ahead of their bodies, longing for the first moment of their lips meeting and finding the warmth and intimacy they craved.

Shelly smothered a gasp. She was remembering the fierceness of Aidan's kisses. He could never have enough of her mouth, kissed her till she was shaken and without thought, weak with longing, being devoured by his desire.

'Shelly? Are you all right?'

'I'm coming,' she said faintly. 'Give me five minutes.'

She put down the receiver, pulled on a bra and pants, and struggled into the first garments that came to hand—polka-dot printed leggings and a sleeveless denim shirt. She shook her hair free and sprayed perfume on her throat. Then she hurried from her cabin, up all the flights of stairs to the promenade deck. The Ensign bar and night-club was the furthest place aft. Outside, the darkened sea was glowing with phosphorescence and dotted with the lights of other ships travelling through the night. The wind tossed her hair across her face as she hurried forward, only remembering now that she had no shoes on.

Aidan came out of the shadows and stopped her passage. His face was dark, etched against the lights of the bar, the music coming from the open doorway. They were playing 'Lady in Red' and he took her in his arms and it was as if he had never been away. He folded her hand against his chest, holding it there with his wrist. His other hand was firmly against her back, drawing her to him.

'Our song,' he murmured, his eyes glittering in the darkness. 'Remember? Let's dance to it one last time.'

How many times had they danced to this tune, sometimes barely moving or speaking, wrapped closely in each other's arms, absorbing the seductive music into their bones, simply content to be together?

Shelly was tall but she did not reach his shoulder. His head was stooped to hers and he manoeuvred her so that she was tucked against his chin. He'd taken off his black tie and opened the top shirt buttons, and wisps of dark hair gleamed against his skin. He ran his good hand up her bare arm and under her shirt, moulding her shoulder.

'Oh, it feels so good to hold you again,' he whispered against her hair, breathing in her perfume.

Shelly could barely speak. She could not believe

she was in Aidan's arms again, dancing to their favourite song, under the spangled stars on a balmy summer's night like some romantic dream. Perhaps it was a dream. But she could feel his heart beating through the thinness of his silk shirt and knew that every moment was real.

'This is madness,' she said, trembling. 'Don't do this.'

'The most wonderful kind of madness, Shelly. Don't let's spoil things again. Let's just enjoy being together, even if it's only for a few minutes. I've missed you so much,' he said. But his eyes were cool. He was punishing her with memories.

Their steps fitted perfectly even with the swaying of the deck. The *Clipper Countess* was gathering speed now as they voyaged through the darkness. Tomorrow they would reach Lisbon, the first port of call, with a leisurely cruise up the River Tagus to their mooring in the Portuguese capital. But neither of them was thinking of the morrow. All that mattered was the now, this night, this moment.

Shelly leaned on the rail as the ship nosed its way along the River Tagus the next morning. She loved this slow approach to Lisbon, loved all the pretty pastel houses on the hillsides, dreamed about retiring there one day to some little villa above the city.

She wanted to be on deck for the moment when the charm of Lisbon came into full sight, the city opening with a blaze of pink and pearl and apricot houses, the old houses on the front a dazzling white, lines of washing fluttering and flowers spilling from wrought-iron balconies.

High on the hill she could see the Castle of St George. The walls of the fortress had dominated the city and the Tagus since the twelfth century.

She stretched her arms wide. No one would have thought she had danced till long after one that morning. She felt pleasantly tired but ready and glowing for all the day might bring. Most of the passengers would be going ashore on excursions or exploring the city on their own. She might have an easy day.

Aidan had made the time fly with hospital anecdotes and the Bacardi in Shelly's drink had relaxed away her body's tenseness. They were both determined not to rake up any unpleasantness, content to talk little and dance to every track they liked.

And he had left her politely at the door to her cabin with no more than a kiss in the palm of her hand as he had said goodnight. But even that kiss, folded in her hand for safe keeping, had stirred memories that were hard to fight.

'Thank you for dancing with an old crock,' he had said briefly, moving away along the corridor. She'd watched him go, drinking in the tall shape of his retreating figure. Her heart had ached with the impossibility of it all.

She had slept soundly, not even waking when the engines slowed down with their usual noisy throb and the huge five-bladed, twelve-ton propeller churned in protest. Dino, her steward, brought her pot of tea early. He knew she would want to be up early and on deck. But she was not the first. Passengers lined the rails for their first glimpses of Lisbon while others, regardless, jogged round the decks with Lisa, the fitness trainer.

She knew Aidan had joined her at the rail before he even said a word. The warm air was hung with stillness. His presence set off distant alarm bells of danger and Shelly felt a kindling hunger she had not expected. He was wearing navy jeans and a white T-shirt, his muscular arms bare and brushed with dark hair. He leaned towards her like a conspirator, grey eyes full of unspoken accusation. He had not forgotten or forgiven.

'Going ashore to see the sights?'

'Not my turn,' she said primly. 'I'm duty medical officer. Jane and Frances are free today.'

'You'll be dressing my hand this morning, then?' He waggled his bandaged fingers at her.

'Yes. Don't forget we open early when in port—eight a.m. till ten a.m.—so that I can see passengers before they go ashore.' Shelly was determined not to be lulled into any degree of friendliness with Aidan. She did not want him back in her life. Last night had been a mistake.

She deliberately moved a few inches along the rail. He was spoiling her enjoyment of their arrival at Lisbon. 'Now, if you'll excuse me. . .'

'Duty calls.' He nodded.

'Exactly.'

His good hand went automatically to his pocket, then he patted it flat. 'Forgot,' he said wryly. 'I gave up smoking some months ago but I still go for the packet of cigarettes.'

Shelly now realised what was absent from his familiar stance; the unthinking flipping of a cigarette from the packet in his top pocket, stooping his head to light it from a flame, all without looking or being aware of what he was doing. And that had been missing from last night's Aidan.

'I'm glad,' said Shelly with feeling. 'It's very unhealthy.'

'I knew I was smoking too much. When you left me I had nothing else to do.' A flicker of sardonic amusement touched his face. 'There was no alternative.'

Shelly clenched her hands at her sides, her body rigid. 'That's not fair. You can't blame me for everything.'

'Can't I? I think I've every right to blame you for all the trouble you caused me. How do you think I felt when I came back from the States and you'd just disappeared without a word? No one knew where you were. Anything could have happened. You could have been injured, lying in some strange hospital somewhere.'

'I wrote,' she said desperately. 'It was all I could do.'

'Wrote!' He spat the word at her, blazing. 'A note three days later to say you had gone away to think. I think I deserved something better than that after being together for such a long time. You're a cool one, you really are.'

'I thought we had a truce. . .last night,' she despaired.

'I think I'm entitled to an explanation.' He glared at her.

'I had a good reason,' she said, a pang piercing her heart. The agony of that time returned, those weeks of hardly knowing what to say or what to do, when day-to-day living was stretched and fearful. 'It took a lot of thought.'

'I bet it did,' he said cuttingly, his eyes cold. 'Try me, just try me with some of those thoughts, Shelly. I'd like to make some sense out of this nonsense.'

'I'm afraid I haven't time to talk about it now,' said Shelly, clawing for breath to retain some composure. 'This isn't the time or place.'

'You're wrong. This is exactly the right time and the right place, believe me. You can't escape me now unless you jump ship. You've had three years, Shelly! Three years of silence. What was I to think all that time? Was it something I said, something I did? God knows, I thought what we had was perfect. I thought we really had something so special.'

'Good morning, Doctor,' said Avril Scott-Card brightly. She was resplendent in a dazzling white nautical outfit, clinging to the arm of her husband, a portly and balding businessman who was already sweating with the growing heat of the day. She had that shopping look painted on her face. 'Going ashore, Dr Smith?'

'Not this time, Mrs Scott-Card. Next port of call perhaps. When we get to Casablanca. I'd like to see Rabat.' Shelly welcomed the intrusion with alacrity. 'How are you feeling this morning? Would you like to come and see me before you go ashore? No charge. Have this one on the house, or should I say on the ship?'

'Now that's really nice of you, Doctor. Fred and I'll just have a bite of breakfast then I'll pop my head round your surgery door.'

Shelly noted that Fred was certainly going to have more than a bite of breakfast. He carried quite a paunch before him. People always ate too much on a cruise because the food was so good and the choice tempting, but it looked as if he ate and drank too much all year round and was storing up trouble for himself in the future. She wondered if she could drop a hint to his wife.

Aidan had gone. He had that knack of merging with shade, of moving quietly in and out of rooms, of reappearing where least expected. He would have made a good spy or secret-service agent, she thought.

Later, waiting at the dockside, she watched the

stream of passengers going ashore to the waiting coaches. It was quite a steep ascent and even the young and fit could fall or misjudge the slope of the gangway.

She would also attend the lifeboat drill at noon for new members of the crew and stewarding staff. It was important that everyone, even the entertainers, knew exactly what to do once the lifeboats were lowered. They practised with casualties and Shelly would truss up a couple of the crew on stretchers with realistic bandages, splints and neck collars.

Later in the cruise there would be an even more important exercise. Some of the crew would go to a hotel that had a big swimming pool, inflate a rubber dingy and practise what to do if it capsized with people underneath. They had to learn how to right the dingy, initiate rescue procedures and climb aboard. Shelly knew she was down to do this one and was not looking forward to it. She was not at her best underneath a heavy rubber dingy, choking on water.

Shelly had an easy morning with a light surgery, checking on the sprained ankle and seeing two of her wheelchair patients. The young father had gone ashore with his family and an escort, determined not to miss anything despite his handicap. Aidan didn't turn up to have his hand dressed. Or perhaps he had turned up at an odd time and Jane or Frances dressed it?

There were plenty of volunteers for the casualties. The younger men thought it was a lark.

'Do we get the kiss of life, Doctor?'

'No, you don't,' she said briskly. 'In fact you might get a very nasty injection in a very sore place.'

'Is that a promise?' they joked.

Part of the deck was cordoned off and passengers who had stayed on board gathered to watch with cameras and video recorders. Number four lifeboat, an open vessel, was slowly winched down, the crew scrambling to their seats, the two casualties being handled carefully aboard. Shelly was almost turning away when things started to go wrong. The engineer couldn't get the engine to start. It whined and spluttered but there was no life in it. The officer ordered the centre-stacked oars to be used but the stewards were not used to handling oars or rowing. They were more used to carrying trays of early-morning tea and smoothing a tight sheet.

'Everybody sit down!'

'Hands in the boat!'

She hid a smile as the oars flayed wildly in all directions. The engineer shouted at the men but they were finding it hard in their bulky life-jackets to get the oars under control. The passengers thought it a wonderful pantomime and called out words of encouragement.

One oar cut through the air then and landed with a thud across the ear of an officer. Shelly heard a shrill feminine cry. It was one of the officers from the purser's department, a pretty red-haired woman called Alice Weyton. She was holding her head and moaning. There was a mess of blood seeping through her fingers.

Shelly hurried down to Deck E to the medical centre to grab her bag. She had no idea how she was going to get out to the lifeboat and the injured officer. It was drifting about fifty metres towards mid-river, milling around in the glittering water.

'How am I going to reach Officer Weyton? Can you get the lifeboat back?' she asked the officer on duty.

'We're launching one of the motor launches to bring the lifeboat back. You can go out on her. But you'll have to hurry unless you want to swim.'

'Not dressed for swimming. Let's get a move-on.'

Shelly hitched up her skirt to her thighs and climbed aboard the launch. It was no time for modesty. But, before she could cover her shapely legs, Aidan was climbing in.

'I think you might need some help with this one,' he said. There was a steely determination in the way he sat down and folded his arms, protecting his bandaged hand as the launch was winched down jerkily.

'I don't need you or your help. And you made it very clear this morning that our truce is pretty fragile.'

'Any truce is fraught with danger. It's only a temporary cessation of something unpleasant, an agreement to stop fighting. And now is hardly the moment for a petty squabble,' Aidan reminded her.

'I haven't the time or the patience for playing games,' said Shelly bluntly. 'There's a wounded officer over there.'

'Head wounds are tricky. Two doctors are better than one in a rocking boat. And I'm wearing jeans, which is a distinct advantage.' He was cleaning his glasses as if he did not have a care in the world.

Shelly acknowledged the sense of his offer. She didn't like head wounds. They frightened her, though of course she tried not to show her fear. But Aidan would know; he would remember from their days working together at Kingham General. She would value some help and opinion. If only it wasn't Aidan Trent sitting so calmly opposite her in the launch! She faced the coming injury with a mixture of calm and dread.

'All right, but just this once,' she said. 'I am in charge here and it's my medical centre on ship and these are my patients. Do you understand that, Aidan? It was all over between us a long time ago. You and I. . .we're yesterday's news.'

CHAPTER THREE

CASABLANCA dockyard was a mass of giant orange cranes, containers being loaded on or off cargo ships, and trucks, vans and lorries crawling along the dusty dock spurs. The city was hung with a heat haze. Sleek steel-grey Moroccan navy vessels were anchored on the far side, sailors swarming over the decks. The *Clipper Countess* lay still at her berth among all the bustle with the quiet elegance of a born lady.

Shelly stood on deck waiting to leave. She had given herself the afternoon off and planned to take the shuttle bus to the United Nations Square and stroll the streets of Casablanca. She watched the passengers filing off the ship to the waiting coaches for the various excursions. A tall man in white shirt and trousers was waving at her vigorously from the dockside. She ignored him.

She was wearing a swirling safari-print skirt with a plain raspberry short-sleeved jacket, both calculated not to offend the Islamic religion. So many tourists went ashore in beach shorts or suntops, despite the dress guidance offered in the port-of-call leaflets delivered to their cabins.

'Come on,' said Aidan, grasping her arm. He'd obviously run up the main stairs, his chest

42

heaving. 'They won't wait forever. The coach is ready to leave.'

'I don't know what you're talking about,' said Shelly, shrugging off his hand. 'I'm not going on any coach.'

'Yes, you are. I booked you a place on the trip to Rabat. Didn't you get my note? I thought you ought to see Rabat. Now, don't argue, girl; after all, it is the capital. I can see you are about to give me a dozen reasons why you can't come. OK, I'm listening.'

'It's a long trip north!'

'Five hours. But they won't sail without you.'

'I shouldn't go so far away from my patients. . .' she faltered.

'Have you got trained staff on board or not? Nothing is going to happen that they can't cope with. Don't you ever go off duty?'

'Who's talking? I can remember a certain consultant going back to the hospital after an operation, and checking on his patient not once but several times during a night,' said Shelly with spirit. Aidan was a dedicated surgeon from operating table to the day a patient went home. 'Didn't you have trained staff? Weren't you ever off duty?'

Aidan growled something unintelligible under his breath. 'I've got you a ticket. If you don't come, I'll take Elaine. She'd like it.'

'Elaine?' The name rang a bell. 'Elaine who?'

'A very nice lady who is travelling on her own. I met her in the library.'

The mouse, thought Shelly. The quiet lady at her dining table who hardly said a word. So Aidan had met her, knew her name, would enjoy her company. The pang was a frisson of jealousy. She tried not to be intimidated by his closeness, while the look Aidan gave her was as private as sleep.

'Please come to Rabat,' he went on, his voice low and gravelly. 'I need protection from the widows. I'm being pursued.'

'Are you sure? You kept out of my way all yesterday.'

'I'm very sure. Come and see how they live in Rabat. It'll be an eye-opener.'

'You mean the luxury of the King's Palace.'

'No, I mean little girls as young as five and six weaving carpets for a living.'

She was already following him down the stairs to the open gangway from Deck C. The Moroccan courier was waiting on the dockside in a flowing white robe, his face wreathed in smiles.

'How much you want for this bag?' he asked as Shelly climbed on the coach. It was a classy Marks & Spencer tote bag, slung over her shoulder.

'I'm sorry,' she said. 'I can't sell it. I haven't got another one.' He shrugged in reply.

There were two places left on the coach. Aidan pushed her into the window seat. She could not believe they were sitting so close, her knee brush-

ing his, his bare arm touching the skin of her arm.
For a moment she allowed herself a grateful smile.
It was a long time since she had been out with a
man and she longed for this kind of intimacy,
something in public, something tender and small
such as his hand reaching up to adjust the air-
conditioning, seeing that she was comfortable,
making sure the sun was not blinding her through
the window.

She didn't deserve this attention or kindness.
But then, Aidan was a caring man. And she had
thrown all that away.

'There,' he said with some satisfaction as they
sped through the endless dusty fawn suburbs of
Casablanca. 'Aren't you glad you came with me?'

'I was going to walk round the city. Take photographs of the watersellers with their big red hats
and brass cups and goatskins of water.'

'They'd probably charge you. Besides, all that
fuel pollution, that chaotic city traffic. . .! To say
nothing of the maniacs ignoring the zebra
crossings. You'd have been coughing yourself silly
in three hours.'

The road left the industrial suburbs and drove
through the poor areas where home was a corru-
gated-iron shack or a squalid hovel for the
teaming millions. Shelly felt the usual pang of
guilt; that she should live in such floating comfort
when human misery was so apparent. She had
heard of the bread riots in Casablanca.

'Not too many white houses here,' she said,

referring to the literal translation of Casablanca.
'Yet they spent three hundred and twenty-five
million pounds on building the new Hassan II
Mosque on the waterfront.'

'Wait till you see it at night,' said Aidan, not
condoning or criticising the vision of the builders,
the gift of a grateful nation to their king. 'They
say it's an amazing sight. The laser beams actually
reach Mecca.'

The street carts were loaded with fresh fruit—
dates, grapes, peaches and huge watermelons.
Already Shelly was dry-mouthed and wished she
had taken the port lecturer's advice and brought
a can of soft drink. They were driving past a
totally flat landscape, vineyards where the vines
were in orderly lines and well irrigated, but some
plants were stunted and beyond producing a single
drop of Cabernet.

The temperature was rising, heat reflecting off
the sandy fields and long ribbon of road. But the
Moroccan women looked cool enough in their
long colourful kaftans and silver jewellery. Some
wore veils but many wore Western suits and high-
heeled shoes under their Arab robes.

It was a long drive to Rabat but, as soon as
the walled town came into sight, people began to
wake up and start taking photographs. Shelly
could image horsemen galloping across the red-
baked plain to pay homage to the sultan in his
palace. They drove along an avenue lined with
eucalyptus trees, through one of the great city

gates which had once exhibited the heads of defeated rebels.

They came to the twelfth-century Hassan Tower, a huge, magnificently sited, unfinished red-tiled minaret on the crest of a hill commanding views over the river estuary and wide riverside area. Ferries and rowing boats were carrying people across to the opposite shores called Sale.

'Well, I don't intend to count them,' said Shelly, pulling on a shady cotton hat, 'but they say there are three hundred and fifty-odd columns left standing after the earthquake.'

'It's marvellous, marvellous.' Aidan spun round, taking in everything with the awe of a student historian, and then he caught hold of her hand. 'It seems that this conqueror Yacoub el Mansour wanted the whole of his army to be able to worship together after some great Portuguese victory.'

Shelly pulled her hand away. She could not cope with the small intimacy. It reminded her of the time when he had always held her hand.

'But he never lived long enough to finish it. Then there was this awful earthquake that ruined most of his work.'

'You've been reading the port notes.'

'I went to the port lecture.'

The heat coming off the modern flagstones in the great white open space was like a pounding cauldron. Shelly licked the sweat forming on her lips. She longed for a drink.

'Many don't live to see their dreams come true,' said Aidan. His face was sombre. If his words had a double meaning, then he had no intention of showing it.

They turned to the wedding-cake carvings of the modern mausoleum built for Mohammed V, a respected king. The crowds had gathered round it, preferring its white prettiness to the stark height and size of the red medieval tower.

'You need a drink,' he said, touching her moist skin. 'You'll get dehydrated.' He bought cans of lemonade from a nearby hotel bar and Shelly drank gratefully. The coach party followed suit and for a while they all sat in the coolness of the hotel foyer, a fountain spilling water over colourful tiles to ease the heat and put up the sale of drinks.

She saw herself mirrored in the wall opposite. Aidan had moved away to buy more drinks. She looked a lonely figure.

'So you've met Elaine,' said Shelly when he returned. 'She hardly says a word at the table. We can't get anything out of her.'

'Really?' said Aidan casually. 'She talks all right to me. She's shy perhaps but then that's rather nice in a woman.'

But he had chosen to take Shelly to Rabat. Sitting beside Aidan in the coach as they drove towards the old walled Medina, Shelly felt a new warmth and contentment creeping over her and it was not from the heat outside the air-conditioned coach. Surely the cement round her heart was not fracturing or a new love kindling these feelings and responses? There was no place for love in her life now. She looked down at his hands, loosely clasped in his lap, his bandages a reminder of an incident she knew nothing about. Aidan would not give her any details of what had happened though she had asked him several times.

He looked at her, a thoughtful expression in his penetrating grey eyes. 'Penny for them?' he said.

'Why are you being so nice to me?'

'Me? Nice? This is my normal, operational bed-side manner. So what are you thinking about?'

The coach was bumping over cobbles, now driving by a sea wall that sealed off a crowded beach and the high flaking stone walls of the old Medina. She was thrown against him and he jerked his injured hand close to his chest.

'I was thinking it was time they resurfaced their roads,' she said, grasping at anything. A flash of annoyance crossed his face but he swallowed his feelings. Shelly closed her eyes. She would do anything to prevent a repetition of those awful days when she was so alone and it seemed to her that Aidan had deserted her. There was so much unfinished business between them, though she could not forget their glorious moments of passion and even now those memories could melt her bones.

'This is the Old Wool Market,' she added

quickly, 'where the pirates used to sell off their slaves.'

'I know someone I'd like to sell off,' said Aidan. 'Only joking,' he added, raising his hands in defence.

They followed the guide up steps through the walls, uneven steps that smelled of urine and had everyone holding their noses. But the houses glimpsed off the narrow lanes were well kept and colourful behind the tall walls and grilled windows. Children sat on the steps, giggling and grinning but not begging. They looked poor but fed and cleanly clothed. The jewellery and kaftan sellers were following them, sensing quick sales and easy victims. One short, swarthy-skinned young man latched on to Shelly when she dropped behind the group.

'You buy?' he said, jangling an armful of silver necklaces in front of her. 'Look, look, missy. Real Moroccan coins, Berber coins, locket for the writings of the Koran. Look, little lid. Ten dollars.'

Shelly hesitated and that was her mistake.

'The lady doesn't want anything,' said Aidan, returning to her side.

'But she is so beautiful,' said the youth, swiftly turning his attention to Aidan. 'You buy for beautiful lady. Look, this real jewels, real silver. Twenty dollars. Rolex watch, fifty dollars.'

'Your English is very good,' said Shelly, trying to rescue Aidan. 'You should be a guide in Rabat instead of selling jewellery.'

'I am student,' said the young man smoothly.
'I am medical student.'

'Come along,' said Aidan, pushing her ahead of
him along the narrow path. 'You're being conned,
Shelly. If he's a medical student then I'm
Genghis Khan.'

'You're very well preserved,' said Shelly.

They thought they had shaken off the youth
when the party followed their guide through the
light and shadows of the souk, then into the carpet
and rug merchants' shop. Dark-eyed little girls
sat cross-legged on the floor, their fingers deftly
handling the weaving process, following the gaudy
red and blue of the geometrical pattern. Their
small hands also held a sharp knife that sliced
through the wool after each double knot. Shelly
imagined small sliced fingers and flinched visibly.

'Money, money,' said a little girl, sensing sym-
pathy, smiling up with great charm and an
open hand.

'I'll have to give her something,' said Shelly,
fishing in her bag.

Aidan shrugged. 'How can you be sure it won't
go straight to her masters?'

'Cynic.'

It was a long drive back to Casablanca along
the coast road. The beaches, a swarming mass of
people and umbrellas earlier that afternoon, were
now deserted, grey waves washing the flat rocks
and empty sand.

Shelly nearly fell asleep. She'd been up late the

previous night with a couple of cabin calls, one of which had taken longer than expected. The man had complained of chest pains and to be on the safe side she had admitted him to one of the wards. Elderly passengers were always a worry to her.

Her hand loosened its grip on a silver bracelet. The cheap Berber coins were overlapping and strung together with a double chain. Aidan touched her fingers, his face brooding, filled with thoughts of his own.

'So you couldn't resist his sob story,' he said.

Shelly did not answer straight away. She was trying to make sense of her feelings. Aidan's touch could still make her ache even when he was no longer part of her life.

'He asked me where I was going after Rabat,' she said quietly. 'I simply couldn't tell him that I was going back to the ship, to the beautiful *Clipper Countess*, when I knew perfectly well that his life, his home, is so totally different. That he probably couldn't even imagine the luxury and comfort of the *Clipper Countess*.'

'Softy,' he said but the narrow space between them was shrinking with each breath. He leaned towards her and tucked an escaping tendril behind her ear. 'How much did you pay for this string of tin coins?'

'Ten dollars.'

'That must have made his day,' said Aidan drily.

'It helped to make mine,' said Shelly, meaning something quite different. It had been her funny, odd way of thanking fate for a whole afternoon in Aidan's company, something she had never expected to have again. A whole afternoon without recriminations or discord. It had been like a dream emerging from a sea mist.

'There's one of our excursion coaches parked over there. I wonder why it's stopped by the roadside. Do you think something's happened?'

'We're stopping too, so we'll soon find out.'

'Ah, there's a girl lying by the side of the road. Come on, Shelly. It looks as if we're going to be needed.'

Shelly did not question the way that Aidan took immediate charge. They were not on the ship now, so she could hardly object.

As soon as their coach stopped Shelly and Aidan hurried out and crossed over to the teenager. They were surprised to find she was one of the passengers. Shelly had seen her in surgery on the first evening, suffering the usual motion sickness. Now she was far more distressed, gasping and crying, her narrow chest heaving and wheezing, her long hair tumbled and damp.

'I can't. . .breathe. . .' she mouthed.

'She's having an asthma attack,' said Aidan.

'Don't worry. We can help you,' said Shelly, sitting the girl upright into a leaning-forward position to help her to breathe more easily. 'Have you got your Ventolin inhaler with you?'

The girl shook her head. 'Forgot. . .' she gasped.

'She needs a nebuliser,' said Aidan.

'Do you happen to have one on you?' said Shelly evenly. 'And do you have a capsule of salbutamol to use with it?'

Shelly didn't wait for an answer but turned her attention to the girl, placing her hands on the girl's shoulders. She would have to do what she could to help without any available medication.

'It's Nicky, isn't it? I remember you. Now, I want to try and slow down your breathing, so watch my mouth and breathe in and out in time with me. In. . .out. . . That's good, really good. Well done. Slowly and steadily. Not so fast or you'll make your condition worse.'

The girl's breathing was slowing down and she seemed less distressed and a better colour, assured by Shelly's calmness and Aidan's firm support for her back.

'As soon as we get you back to the *Clipper Countess* we'll put you on a nebuliser. It's nothing to be afraid of. It's like your Ventolin but you breathe it in through a mask for ten minutes. Don't worry. We'll get you back safely. I'll stay with you all the way.'

'I want. . .to. . .ship. . .' Nicky started to cry again.

'Of course you do and the sooner the better.' Shelly turned to Aidan. 'I don't think a local hospital would be a good idea. We've no idea of conditions or how long it would take to get attention. We have everything we need aboard and her attack is coming under control.'

'I agree. I've checked with the driver. Another fifteen minutes should have us back at the docks and shipside.' Aidan helped Nicky to her feet. 'Tomorrow I'll teach you some yoga breathing. It's called alternate-nostril breathing and is very easy to learn and can be a great help, Nicky. You'll be able to do it yourself whenever you feel a tightness or a shortness of breath coming on.'

Nicky couldn't speak but she nodded her agreement.

'Has anyone some bottled mineral water?' Shelly made a mental note: never go on a trip without some water. A woman came forward with a bottle of mineral water and Nicky sipped slowly. It all helped.

Shelly stayed with Nicky for the short drive, reassuring her and making sure the attack did not worsen. It was no use telling the girl she should never go anywhere without her inhaler. Lots of asthma sufferers forgot or were ever-optimistic that they would not get another attack.

Back at the dockside by the *Clipper Countess*, they were first off the coach and Nicky was helped aboard. Shelly knew exactly where to put her hands on the plastic bag which contained the sterile nebuliser equipment and a phial of salbutamol. In moments Nicky had the mask over her mouth and nose and the bronchodilator was being inhaled along the green tube. The relief was immediate and her eyes flashed a grateful look as her breathing eased. It always worked so well.

Shelly was relieved. The delay had been unavoidable. An injection of aminophylline in a vein would have been the next step if the attack had not settled.

She put away her equipment as Nicky went back to her cabin to rest, reckoning that that young lady would be down to the second sitting of dinner, though she might not have the energy to dance till one a.m. Asthma attacks were exhausting and took a while to get over.

She checked on her patient with chest pains. He was anxious to get back to his wife and, as he seemed quite stable, she discharged him.

Evening surgery was the usual aftermath of a trip ashore, especially to such a hot place as Morocco. There were insect bites and heat exhaustion, upset tummies and twisted ankles. So many passengers did not take her advice in the daily news-sheet not to drink local cold drinks or buy local ice creams. It was asking for trouble.

Aidan strolled in at the end of surgery.

'Busy evening?' he asked, settling himself at the side of the treatment bed. He had already showered and changed and his hair was wetly slicked back. It was going to be an informal evening with a carnival party on deck and he had on a loudly patterned shirt and crisp white trousers.

'To be expected after excursions and it was very hot,' said Shelly, carefully removing the old dressings. 'This is getting better,' she said, examining the reddened fingers and palm. 'You'll be able to expose it to the air soon. Your skin needs air.'

He peered down at his hand, his eyes narrowed as he flexed the stiffened fingers. He did not say what he really needed; he needed Shelly, but perhaps it was all too late. 'Will I be able to use it again?' His voice strained, as if he was hiding his true emotions.

'Physiotherapy should help,' said Shelly, sounding more cheerful than she felt. 'The new skin will soften. I'll give you some E45 cream to put on it—it does wonders. I'm sure all your flexibility will return and you'll be able to operate again.'

'Good,' he grunted. 'Not quite ready to retire to the country as a GP.'

'Could be worse. Don't knock GPs.'

'Are you coming to the dance on deck tonight?' he asked. 'Moonlight, the stars, steel band. I do a mean samba.'

'You seem to think this job is one long holiday,' said Shelly, chiding him. 'I have to work. This liner is like a village, a small town, bustling with people and activity. I have everyone to look after and accidents happen all the time. The fact that seven hundred of those people change names and ailments every few weeks merely adds to my work load.'

'So why did you leave Kingham General?' he

asked suddenly, taking firm hold of her wrist.
'Tell me. Put me out of my misery.'

Shelly felt a constriction leap into her throat.
He filled the room with his presence. She wanted
to turn back the clock, to return to those ecstatic
days when he had loved her. He did not love her
now. Those clear grey eyes were darkened and
unloving.

She had left Kingham General because she
loved him too much, she remembered, and she
could never have gone on working there, seeing
derision in his eyes every day.

'I left because I had to,' she said carefully.
'Something made it essential that I went. I can't
tell you, Aidan. I'm sorry but it was purely
private.'

'Have you forgotten what we had together? I
thought we didn't have any secrets,' he rasped,
distressed beyond measure. 'More than two whole
years of loving and being so easy with each other's
company. We saw each other almost every day.
It was wonderful. I thought I had found paradise.'

'No, I haven't forgotten,' she breathed. 'How
could I? It isn't fair. . .'

'You were a woman who was equal with me
and I liked that. You were a good doctor, I saw that
immediately. Your work at Kingham General was
excellent in every way and you were well qualified. Your career could have taken off. And you
always looked wonderful and I fell in love with
you. Oh, Shelly, how I loved you. Didn't I ever

tell you? Is that what went wrong? Didn't I tell you enough? I know that women like to be told frequently but I thought that everything I did, every day, told you that.'

Her eyes were filtering tears. She brushed them aside. She couldn't stand this. Three years of being away from Aidan had been healing and that was how she wanted it to stay.

'This is ridiculous,' she said, trying to calm the churning of her heart. 'What we had is all over. It was all over three years ago. I thought I had made that clear.'

'Oh, yes, you made that very clear, my love,' said Aidan bitterly. 'What I want is an explanation. Do you think it's fair that I should not be told why? Do I have to take the blame for something I don't understand?'

Shelly wanted to say, Yes, yes, you take the blame. It was your fault, Aidan. You and your stupid ideals. Instead she suppressed her thoughts with the detachment of a scientist, kept the words locked in her head.

'If you don't mind, I still have a lot of paper-work to do,' she said, taping his bandage securely. 'And I have a security meeting in the purser's office later on this evening.'

'Busy girl. I won't delay you any longer. You've made it very clear that you have no intention of clearing things up between us. Perhaps it's something you're ashamed of.'

He got up abruptly and strode out of her

surgery, seeming even taller than usual, his dark
head thrown back with soundless tension. She had
seen that stance so many times—after a difficult
operation or caring talk with a terminally ill
patient. It was a kind of defence.

Shelly was on the promenade deck when the
Clipper Countess began to pull slowly out of
Casablanca docks. She watched the twenty-mile-
long laser beam shoot from the new Hassan II
Mosque built on the new Corniche sea front. Its
silver beam pointed like a bright finger piercing
the sky and towards Mecca. It would be visible
for hundreds of miles out to sea with its message
saying 'Allah has His throne on the water'.

She turned to watch the dancing round the pool.
Everyone was wearing colourful leis round their
necks and the band was playing Carribean music.
Aidan was dancing with Elaine and it was obvious
that she was flattered by his attentions. He was
dancing with his usual sensual carelessness, his
head bent to listen to what the woman was saying.

Shelly fought down a gulping, incoherent misery. She wanted to be the one dancing with Aidan.
She wanted his hand resting lightly on her hip
bone, moving with the beat of the music. She
wanted the promise of kisses on the deck afterwards, in his arms and under the stars.

A thin veil of cloud had formed in the darkened
sky and was drifting across the crescent moon.
Suddenly it seemed very right that they should
have this one last chance to be together. She

STELLA WHITELAW   61

would ask him for a dance. After all, they had
a truce.

But he had gone. So had Elaine. The music
played on and the crowd of happy passengers were
snaking round the tables to a conga rhythm. A
cold breeze struck her shoulders through her thin
shirt as the *Clipper Countess* nosed her way
towards the Atlantic, setting a southwesterly
course for the Canaries once clear of the coast.

Carnival streamers were being thrown down
from the upper decks and the dancers moved in
a swirl of fluttering paper as lights like fountains
lit the scene with changing colours.

Shelly turned away. She shivered as she
remembered the rough friction of his hair against
her smooth silkiness, her fingers tangling in his
dark curls. She longed for the soft rasp of his
thumbs on her breasts and the way his arms used
to fold her to him.

She stared hopelessly down at the dark,
hostile water.

CHAPTER FOUR

SHELLY was awoken by her bleeper going off at three-twenty a.m. She reached out for it and the operator put her straight through to a cabin on Deck A.

'Hello, this is Dr Smith,' she said, trying to bring some alertness into her voice. 'How can I help you?'

'Doctor, please come quickly. My wife's in terrible pain. Hurry.'

'Where is the pain?'

'In her chest and left arm.'

Shelly was already sliding out of bed, pulling down her cotton nightshirt, which had wrinkled up as she had slept. Her medical bag was always at hand. She struggled into a man's navy silk dressing gown, which she had bought to pass as a uniform for middle-of-the-night emergencies.

'Give me your name and cabin number,' she said.

'Mr and Mrs Harris. Cabin number A 34. And hurry, please. She's very bad.'

'I'm on my way.'

Shelly took the lift to the first passenger deck and ran along the corridor. Mr Harris was peering out of his cabin door, his dressing gown hastily tied, his sparse grey hair standing on end.

'In here, in here,' he said urgently.

Gwen Harris was sitting up in bed in a pink nightdress, pressing her hand to her chest and her arm, looking ill and anxious. Her skin was pale and she was sweating. It did not take Shelly long to diagnose an attack of angina. There was pain behind the breast bone, down her left arm, up into the jaw and down into the abdomen. She couldn't speak. Her temperature and pulse were normal and she was breathing at eighteen to the minute, a little up. Her breathing was constrained but she was not short of breath.

'Has this happened before?' Shelly asked, giving Mrs Harris a 0.5mg tablet of glyceryl trinitrate. 'Suck this slowly under your tongue, Mrs Harris.'

'Well. . .a little pain sometimes. . .but nothing as bad as this,' said Mr Harris, hovering.

'Has Mrs Harris been to her own doctor?'

'Er. . .no. We didn't think it was necessary.'

'I think it is necessary now that your wife should see her doctor as soon as you get home. There's no need to panic. We can contain the angina with medication while Mrs Harris is aboard the *Clipper Countess*.'

Mrs Harris's colour was returning and she was breathing more easily. It was obvious that the pain was being relieved.

Shelly took her hand and held it comfortingly. 'This pain is a warning, Mrs Harris. It means you must take things a bit easier. It could have been brought on by a heavy meal and we all know what the food is like aboard. Or perhaps some exertion you're not used to or a strong emotion?'

'We did have a bit of a row,' said Mr Harris. 'It was nothing really. About sending postcards to all and sundry. Gwen's nutty about sending postcards home and I think it's all a load of rubbish.'

Shelly picked up the phone and dialled the room-service number. She ordered a tray of tea from the steward on duty.

'No more rows, if possible. Have a nice restful cruise and no rushing about on strenuous excursions,' she smiled. 'No heavy meals. Try to choose a light menu, Mrs Harris. If you're feeling emotional or tense, take one diazepam tablet three times a day. I'll give you a prescription and your husband can collect them from the medical centre in the morning.'

'Thank you very much, Doctor. I'm feeling. . . better already,' said Mrs Harris, lying back on the pillow.

'Has the pain gone?'

'Almost.'

'When it's gone, take out what's left of the glyceryl trinitrate and throw it away. They can give you a headache and you don't want that after what you've been through.'

She left the couple having a cup of tea. She wandered along the empty corridor, tightening the sash round her slender waist, pushing back her tousled hair. The vibration from the ship's engines was hardly discernible on Deck A but nothing was going to keep Shelly from going back to sleep. It would be surprising if she reached her cabin without dozing off on the way.

'Sleepwalking?' Aidan asked. He appeared from nowhere and looked dreadful. His lei was crushed and disintegrating as if it had been subject to a great deal of pressure, and he was shoeless. Shelly could guess how the flowers had got crushed. She felt a pang of jealousy and an immense loneliness, remembering how he had left the pool area with Elaine.

'Carrying my bag?' she replied with sarcasm. 'It's four o'clock in the morning. I had a cabin call. What are you doing up at this hour? Changing cabins?'

'Nasty. Well below the belt,' said Aidan coldly. 'Not like you at all, Doctor.'

Shelly was immediately contrite. 'I'm sorry, Aidan. I'm tired and confused. And, of course, it's none of my business. If you want a little shipboard romance then it's part of your holiday package and good luck to you.'

'I do not want a little shipboard romance.' He glared, snatching her bag from her hand. 'I want you—as you used to be. Not the smart, cool professional you've become, in a cushy job, drinking with the customers.'

'This is not a cushy job,' said Shelly indignantly. 'What GP could be called out any night of the week for weeks on end? People always feel worse in the small hours, you should know that. Any pain or discomfort prays on the imagination and becomes life-threatening in the middle of the night. But Mrs Harris had a mild angina.'

'How is Gwen Harris?'

'You know her?'

'She's at my dining table. They were cutting a rug on the dance floor tonight.'

'What?' Shelly looked puzzled. 'You mean they were dancing?'

'Jiving. Straight from the forties. Reliving their youth. They were really good.' He gave a little demonstration in the corridor. Shelly couldn't stop herself laughing. It was impromptu fun, so unlike the aloof Aidan she had once known. It produced a kind of ache, a longing to be carefree and happy again.

'They didn't tell me anything about jiving,' said Shelly. 'No wonder Mrs Harris had a touch of angina. She must be in her late sixties.'

'But she's still a teenager at heart and wanting to dance to the music of their youth,' said Aidan, taking her arm. 'Doctor, you need your bed or else you won't be fit for tomorrow. It's clay-pigeon shooting on the lower deck. Bound to be lots of casualties.'

'Today,' Shelly yawned. 'You, too. . .couldn't you sleep?' There was no way Aidan had been with Elaine, she knew that now.

'No, my mind wouldn't settle down. So I played

a little blackjack, took a walk, got some fresh air.' He steered her towards the medical centre. 'But don't worry about me, I can catch up on deck. I'll find a lounger in some quiet spot and I can sleep from meal to meal. All day at sea. . .I think that's what I like best. The voyaging from port to port.'

'So do I,' said Shelly as they went down flight after endless flight of mirrored stairs. She leaned on him a little, enjoying his support. 'Just sea and more sea and more sea.'

Aidan slipped his arm round her waist, his mouth turning with humour and a fleeting gentleness. He fingered her belted waist. 'And this is a very dangerous outfit to be walking around in during the lonely night. Very fetching too. What happens if I tug at this?'

'Nothing,' said Shelly, pleating the soft fabric. 'I'm holding on to the other end. And it's not a lonely place at night. The crew are still working, the bridge is manned, and the kitchen, make an early start, especially the bakers. A vast army of cleaners is making everywhere spic and span for the coming day. How could I possibly feel lonely with all that going on?'

'This is your cabin,' he said, stopping, his eyes glittering.

'I know.' There was a milky stillness to the air. He was waiting for her to say something.

'Are you going to ask me in?' he asked huskily, with a savage indrawn breath.

'No,' she said, deliberately slowing her breathing, her body saying something quite different.

'That's not very friendly.'

'You've just told me off for socialising with the customers,' said Shelly, backing away. Aidan was moving closer, then his hand skimmed her spine with an electrifying touch. He drew her slowly towards him. She felt her pulse beginning to sky-rocket but she could not resist the gentle pressure that was arousing responses in her.

He was interpreting her silent demand. She was half asleep but her body was blossoming slowly. Why not? Life could be wonderful and she had been alone for so long.

His mouth shifted from her hair to her neck, to the soft curve of her shoulder where the collar of the robe had moved and bared her skin. Shelly stroked down his back, timidly at first, afraid of what they might be starting. But he tensed and groaned softly.

'Don't do that,' he groaned. 'I can't stand it.'

But she wanted to let her hands roam over him. He had the most beautiful male body she had ever seen, so strong and muscled, without an ounce of fat on his long, lean length. She remembered his welcomed weight on her and desire flared up in her like a grass fire out of control.

Soundlessly his mouth reached for her lips and they were locked in a kiss that went on and on and on. The world swirled round them; walls disappeared, the ship vanished, the air held them in a vacuum that was drenched with almost forgotten love and longing.

They gathered each other more closely, shivering with pleasure, kisses deepening into subtle exploration as if they had never kissed before. She was in a trance of despair. She had never wanted this to happen but now it was too late.

Shelly felt she was being absorbed by him and did not care. His tongue was probing and caressing her mouth, swallowing her juice, and her body was melting in a hot whirlpool of joy. This was her Aidan, loving her again. He could not kiss like this without love. His mouth said, I love you. His body, closely welding each curve to hers, said, I love you.

She let her hands move round his neck and touch the softness of his hair, newly washed, so like a child's.

For a moment the thought stunned her. And her body quivered. A child's hair. Their child. She clung to him, her bloodstream singing with love for him and mourning the child she had lost. Their baby. Their tiny baby boy that he knew nothing about.

The tears were wet on her cheeks and he kissed them away tenderly, tasting their sweetness, remembering times before when she had cried and he had comforted her with lovemaking that stilled her fears. Now he was not sure what to do. He was afraid of her and the hurt she could inflict.

'Don't cry, my darling,' he said hopelessly. 'I

didn't mean to make you cry. Oh, Shelly, please
don't cry. I can't stand it. Darling, my love, my
own sweet love. . .'

He buried his face in her hair, drinking in the
scent with an open mouth, wanting her desperately, not caring what had gone terribly wrong,
only knowing that she was the only woman he
wanted; that their love had been priceless and
they had thrown it away.

Shelly hung her head so that he would not see
the truth in her eyes—that she still loved him and
her body still longed for him. If he touched her
intimately she would be lost.

'I have to get some sleep,' she murmured.

'Of course. See you in the morning.'

They wrenched their bodies apart and Shelly
opened her door, every pore, every nerve tingling.
She fell on to her bed and clutched her breasts,
wanting to stop their tumultuous and swollen
frenzy of feeling. She wanted something, a cold
shower, anything to bring her to her senses.
Instead her bleeper went off.

She reached for it. 'Dr Smith,' she breathed
raggedly. 'How can I help you?'

It was four a.m. and she had to go on another
call. A passenger travelling on his own, who had
been on the day-long excursion to Marrakesh, had
sampled everything going at a belly-dancing café
club. He had been found unconscious by his steward. That the dancing had been in the middle of
the afternoon had made no difference; he had

drunk every kind of drink in sight, his thirst increased by joining in the frenetic belly-dancing, and he was now paying for it.

'She was v'r beau'ful,' he confided to Shelly, over and over again. 'Sho beau'ful. . .' The man had passed out in his bathroom, where his steward had found him when answering a service call. The steward had alerted the medical centre, concerned that it might be more than drunkenness.

'And what did you have to drink in this night-club?' asked Shelly, getting the man into bed with the help of the steward. The man was finding it difficult to walk or talk; his face was flushed and his eyes bloodshot.

'Dunno. They just kept. . .bringing more. B'ful girl, Doctor. . .' He hiccuped. 'Jus' s'wonderful. . .'

'Drink this, please,' said Shelly, pouring out a glass of water from the iced jug. 'And another. We'll wash all those toxic concoctions out of you.'

'Did I do right to call you, Doctor?' the steward asked anxiously.

'Of course, you did well,' she reassured him. 'It could so easily have been something else. Unconsciousness could be several other conditions. But this is plain intoxication and alcoholic dehydration. Get Mr Milton to drink plenty of water and then let him sleep it off. I don't think he'll put in an appearance at breakfast.'

'I'll keep an eye on him.'

'Thank you, Ahmed. I really can't stay with

him. I must get some sleep but call me if you're
worried, especially if he starts choking.'

Shelly found it hard to go back to sleep. She
dozed fitfully. It was a relief to drink her early-
morning tea and shower quickly. She had no
appetite for breakfast but knew she must eat
before the morning surgery. Aidan's kisses were
still imprinted on her mouth and her skin and it
was difficult to concentrate with her thoughts
dazed and going wild.

She could not face a formal cooked breakfast
in the dining-room and opted for the buffet-style
breakfast offered on the pool deck. She joined
the queue, smiling but not talking, and helped
herself to slices of melon and pineapple, a hot
croissant and a cup of black coffee.

She sat as far away from anyone as possible,
at a sheltered table behind some palms, with only
a distorted view of the passing waves. Passengers
were wonderful but they did have a habit of talking personal medical matters, parading ailments,
hoping for words of wisdom to drop from her lips.

But even her breakfast did not go undisturbed.
She heard a cry of anguish from the central area
of the deck.

Shelly gulped down her coffee and left her
unfinished croissant. A woman in shorts and
T-shirt lay at the foot of the steps, clutching her
ankle. Her breakfast tray was all over the place,
broken china and spilt coffee rolling and spreading
over the deck.

'All right, everyone. Don't crowd round. I'll see to this lady. Where does it hurt?'

'My ankle, my ankle, it's agony. . .' Her face was screwed up with pain. 'Oh, Lord. . .what have I done?'

'I've said time and time again that passengers should be helped down the steps with their trays,' said Shelly, going down on her knees to examine her and not caring who heard. She would have to bring it up again at their next health and safety meeting. 'That's what the stewards are for. It's hard enough walking down the steps when the ship is tilting, let alone carrying a laden tray.'

The ankle was swelling up fast. Shelly used a high pad of pool towels to lift the foot and rest it. She removed the woman's sandal and had a feeling that this was not an ordinary sprain. A second swelling was covering the area of the fifth metatarsal, one of the thin bones of the foot below the toes. It could be a fracture.

'You're going to need an X-ray,' said Shelly. 'But don't worry. We'll get you down to the medical centre without causing too much of a drama. I'll phone for a wheelchair to take you down.'

'So stupid,' the woman moaned.

'No, not stupid,' said Shelly. 'An unfortunate accident. It could have happened to anyone. Blame it on a quartering sea.'

A cushy job? Aidan's words came back to her in the middle of a busy morning. Morning surgery stretched till midday. Jane did Aidan's dressing at some point and Shelly did not see him.

The X-ray revealed a hairline fracture in the woman's fifth metatarsal. It needed frequent cold pads and firm crêpe bandaging. Shelly reassured the woman that she would be a heroine and hopping round the ship on crutches in no time.

'You can go on excursions but don't overdo it,' she advised.

'I don't go on the excursions,' said the woman, looking at her clumsy foot with dismay. 'I stay on board the ship and pretend it all belongs to me.'

Shelly smiled. She knew the feeling. Sometimes passengers acted as if the beautiful liner belonged to them. It produced a glow of pride and ownership that became a special dream.

'How very wise,' said Shelly. 'You'll have a lovely time and everyone will wait on you hand and foot.'

Shelly took a breath of air before lunch, strolling the decks, but she knew she was really looking for Aidan, trying to find his hiding place for a snooze. But when she found him she did not like what she saw.

Elaine was slowly stroking suntan lotion across his broad shoulders while he rested his head on his arms, eyes closed. The expression on his face was one of contentment.

Shelly felt a surge of anger. She wanted to snatch the bottle out of Elaine's hand and toss it over the side. Instead she clenched her fingers hard into the palms of her hands, biting on her lip.

Elaine was looking pleased with herself, her mouth in a satisfied smile. Well, she would, wouldn't she? Aidan was such an attractive man, such good company, always fun. And he had chosen her, a little brown shrimp, to be his companion on this cruise. It was enough to turn any woman's head.

Shelly averted her eyes from the sight of his almost naked body and the long tanned legs, the shapely feet, the sexy buttocks in navy swimming briefs. She wanted to elongate herself beside that long body, to feel it fit into her curves and mould herself to his shape.

Her appetite fled. She skipped lunch and went to the bow of ship where the crew had deck area. There were no loungers for the crew for sunbathing. She took a big towel, peeled off shorts and shirt and lay down in the sun in her bikini. She did not want to sleep, just doze. It wasn't safe to fall asleep—that was when passengers and crew got burnt, or at least unwanted strap marks in the wrong places. She remembered one passenger who had fallen asleep with a baseball cap half over her face and had had to disguise a clown's face for the rest of the cruise.

The sun's warmth on her body was deeply relaxing. She stretched like a cat, wriggling her toes and fingers, letting thoughts of Aidan's kisses and his well-remembered mouth colour her dreams. The sound of the ocean was soothing, a lullaby of rushing waves with the distant throb of the powerful engines far below.

That afternoon at Rabat had been an unexpec-
ted oasis of pleasure, simply being with him,
walking by his side, enjoying his splendid height
with sideways glimpses of his fine dark head, their
hands brushing accidentally. And he had taken
her hand several times as if nothing had ever happened, and they were back in the carefree days
of their romance at Kingham General, the sun
glinting on his glasses.

Those days sent a quiver through her. Their
first dinner date had been punctuated with awk-
wardness and embarrassment on her part. She had
been a junior doctor finishing her first year; Aidan
the hospital's most respected consultant surgeon.
It was a wonder that he ever asked her out again.
But he did, gently and tenderly easing her shy-
ness, making her laugh. He knew what he wanted.
He knew that Shelly was the only woman for him.

'I knew from the first moment I saw you,
darling,' he said ardently, a long time later when
she was captive in his arms in the warmth of the
night. 'Just one look. That's all it needed.'

'. . .that's all it needs. . .'

It was like an echo from the past. The same
voice, almost the same words. Shelly was awake
in an instant. She sat up cautiously, unashamedly
listening.

'I don't want to worry you, Captain Bellingham,
but trauma works in funny ways.' Aidan's voice
came clearly through the air from the bridge

above. He sounded the cool and professional medical man. 'It's unpredictable.'

'I'll make arrangements to have her watched,' said Captain Bellingham. 'We don't want an incident on board ship. You're quite sure, aren't you, Mr Trent?'

'Oh, yes, she's unstable. I could give you time and place but it might confuse matters. . .'

Their voices grew fainter as they walked further away on the deck above. But then Shelly heard her own name. She was stunned. There was no doubt about it. They were talking about her.

CHAPTER FIVE

THE *Clipper Countess* anchored early morning off shore of the southern Jandia region of the island of Fuerteventura, one of the lesser known of the Canary Islands, but gaining in popularity since the discovery of its miles of golden beaches. From the top deck Shelly thought it looked a barren place with rolling and eroded brown hills and a few ribbons of roads, scrub and stone, and very little habitation.

She had passed up on the last two ports of call, even though the tiny port of Santa Cruz de la Palma, the capital of La Palma, had looked so attractive with its long streets of colourful balcon-ied merchants' houses. It was one of the least developed of the Canary Islands.

Jane and Frances had come back with armfuls of inexpensive souvenirs, flowers from the market and photos of the massive cement model of the *Santa Maria*, Colombus's famous ship. For some reason the citizens had built the ship in the middle of their picturesque town and turned it into a museum. Most of the passengers endured the sharp twisting roads up the spine of mountains to see the still smoking volcano, Caldera de Taburiente, with its vast crater the size of a small park.

Shelly stayed on board, still smarting from Aidan's treacherous remarks to Captain Bellingham. She could hardly believe what she had heard. How could he have told Captain Bellingham something so personal, and so distressing to her, when he did not know the real truth? And she had no intention of putting the record straight with the good captain. What happened to her before joining the crew of the *Clipper Countess* was her own business.

She kept out of Aidan's way, beginning to know his haunts on ship, the upper-deck wing where he liked to sunbathe, the Ensign, his favourite bar for a pre-dinner drink, the blackjack tables, the library where he often browsed. She did not want to see him or bump into him by accident.

'Traitor,' she seethed under her breath. 'How dare he?'

But she had watched Aidan and Elaine going ashore at Santa Cruz, walking together along the short length of mole which led straight into town, followed their route across the tree-lined square till she lost sight of them in the maze of streets. It had hurt, especially when she saw Elaine's rapt face, looking up at Aidan, hanging on his every word.

Today was different. Shelly knew she deserved a break. She did not let her staff work non-stop.

The thirteen-mile endless beaches of southern Fuerteventura were long enough for anyone to get lost. With luck, she wouldn't see a soul she knew; she could pretend she was a German tourist, speak to no one. She would walk a few miles until she found some secluded patch of sand, and then she would swim and swim until it was time to catch the last launch returning to the ship. She missed having a good swim. The crew pool on the *Clipper Countess* was hardly built for swimming. Three strokes and she had reached the other side. Sometimes she swam round and round the pool till she felt like a goldfish.

She went on one of the first launches before most of the passengers had finished their breakfasts. She wore an ankle-length black patterned sarong over her bikini, dark sunglasses and a man's bleached straw hat. Hardly the gear for climbing aboard a rocking launch, but it was a good disguise. Yet the officer manning the launch still recognised her as she was helped aboard.

'Good morning, Doctor,' he said. He was a smart young man in white shirt and shorts, long white socks, cap set straight on his head, hands on the steering wheel, waiting for the launch to fill up.

'Good morning, John. How's the new baby?'

'Growing,' he grinned. 'Getting to be a handful.'

The launch was riding a swell. Other early birds were finding it difficult to time the right moment to step aboard. Shelly hoped no one had an accident. That would put a stop to her swim.

The ship was dressed overall with flags streaming in the strong wind. There was an air of excitement everywhere. This was not a day of culture and sightseeing but a day for pure relaxation and sun-worshipping.

It was already warming up, the sea sparkling with facets of a million watery diamonds. There would be little shade on the beaches and it was a day for some prime burning casualties at evening surgery.

The launch took them across the short expanse of sea to a floating pontoon that lead to a rocky headland. It was like walking a wobbly plank. A bus waited to ferry them round the headland to the glorious beaches. Here was a small complex of houses, apartments and hotels, all white and hot pink, to make up for the lack of flowers. A few dusty palm trees provided token shade.

Already the serious sunbathers were staking their patches with umbrellas and beach chairs and stripping off. In the distance was a solitary lighthouse. Shelly decided to walk as far as the lighthouse, timing the distance. She would be able to keep the *Clipper Countess* in sight, though that would hardly be of any use to her if she saw the floating beauty sailing away in the late afternoon.

'At last,' she sighed with anticipation. 'Here I come, sea.'

She took off her sandals and waded through the shallow water. It was wonderful. The sea was already warm and the little wavelets tickled her toes. She swung her bag, suddenly feeling young

and carefree for once. Her sick patients were in
good hands, Aidan was. . .well, she hadn't the
slightest idea where Aidan was, nor did she care.
Perhaps they would stay on board. She did not
feel the fragrant Elaine was keen on swimming
or sunbathing. She had never seen the woman in a
swimsuit or shorts. Elaine always wore full-skirted
cotton sundresses and lots of white jewellery.

Shelly was used to seeing naked bodies but not
quite so many and all at once. The young and
slimly tanned looked lovely, with or without
clothes, but some of the beer bellies were not a
pretty sight. Still, even the old and overweight
had a right to air their skin to the warmth of the
sun and she had to admire their courage and lack
of embarrassment.

By the time she had reached the lighthouse
Shelly felt she had walked far enough. The crowds
had thinned and there was plenty of spare sand.
She spread out her towel, unwound her sarong
and lay down, pulling aside the straps of her bikini
bra. She had brought fruit and water in her tote
bag, enough to last the day that lay ahead.

She stretched out her arms and let the sand run
through her fingers. If only Aidan could be beside
her. In their time together, they had never been
able to go away for a holiday. The most they
had been able to do was to snatch rare weekends
at the Sussex coast and then it had always rained.

'Aidan, Aidan, where did you get your cracked-
brain ideas? I always knew you were idealistic,

but how could you let it spill over into our life?'
The words were locked into her head. She had
said them a hundred times to herself during the
last three years. Aidan had not wanted children.
The planet was already over-populated. By the
next century, it would be a teeming mass of people
reproducing. . .

Slowly she smoothed suntan lotion over her
shoulders, legs and vulnerable stomach. Even
after weeks at sea and an even honey-tan, she
was still careful.

She would be glad when this cruise was over
and Aidan returned to his life and let her get on
with hers. Only a few more ports of call—
Madeira, Gibraltar, Bordeaux—and then the
Clipper Countess would be heading for home.
Shelly was due twenty-four hours' leave once they
reach Southampton and she looked forward to
seeing her mother.

Her first swim was bliss. She swam out a good
way, then lay on her back in the warm water,
blinking against the sun, paddling around. There
were other swimmers but they all seemed a long
way off.

She loved the feel of the water on her skin.
Before she knew what was happening, she was
taking off the top of her bikini and tucking the
scrap of material into the band of her bikini pants.
The water was like silk, soft and caressing. The
feeling was sensuous and her breasts rose, floating
on the surface of the water like rosebuds.

Shelly didn't care. No one could see her. She could swim and swim, topless if she wanted, and enjoy the wonderful feeling, the freedom, knowing how her ancestors had once felt. They hadn't worn swimsuits or clothes. She was at peace, her cares leaving her, her love for Aidan still close in her heart, making her nipples tingle.

'Hey, do I recognise this little mermaid? Say cheese for the camera.'

It was too late. Aidan was swimming towards her, water spilling off his dark hair, his eyelashes glued and spiky as if he had swum a long way. He trod water, not far from her, his gaze skimming her naked breasts, approving, admiring, wondering what she would do now.

'Camera?' she shrieked, sinking under, spluttering, finding she was out of her depth.

'Only teasing.'

'There's no law,' she said defiantly, splashing about, not knowing where to go, what to do.

'Don't cover yourself, my love. You look beautiful, like a water nymph. Please don't be embarrassed. I love seeing you so natural. You look wonderful. Happy and relaxed for once. All the tiredness has gone from your face. I'll go away, if you really want me to,' he said tenderly, dazzling her with his kindness. 'But please don't send me away. I'd much rather stay. Do you really want me to go?'

'No, don't go.' Her voice was full of desperation. She wanted him to stay.

He moved closer behind her, slipping his arms round her waist. 'Then I won't go, Shelly. This is for us. This day is for us. I need this time with you. Let's just enjoy it. Everyone else is enjoying themselves.'

She leaned back against him, revelling in the feel of his naked hair-roughened chest, the firm hips against hers, the long legs touching hers as she tried to tread water and not sink under the waves.

'Don't struggle, Shelly. I can reach the sea bed. I'm standing on firm sand. I'll hold you. Relax back against me; put your head on my shoulder. Trust me, let go, let me take you with me,' he said, his lips skimming her shoulder, tasting the salt.

The sea's foam was gushing and tumbling against their skins. She blinked with unseeing eyes up into the unseamed sky, the endless blue, her smile folded into eternity. Flesh caressed flesh. Their skins were as soft as silk, his muscles as strong as steel. Her blood rang with melodies as old as time. It was almost impossible to restrain the urgency that surged through her veins.

'Aidan,' she breathed, knowing it was dangerous. 'I don't mean any of this.'

'My darling, I don't care what you mean. It's enough that you are in my arms again.'

He moved his hands caressingly over her breasts and for a moment Shelly quivered anew against the wiry hair of his chest. She was held captive

by her longing for his touch. Then she
remembered with clarity.

'Aidan, your hand! You mustn't get it wet.'

'All clear. I've decided the bandages can come
off. As you said, it needs air now and today that's
what it's getting.' He waved his left hand in front
of her. The skin was pink and new but healthy-
looking.

'I'm so pleased for you.' She smiled radiantly,
turning in his embrace and throwing her arms
round his neck. The roughness of his chest against
her breasts was intoxicating. She was feeling quite
light-headed.

'Hold on a moment, Doctor,' said Aidan,
laughing, swinging her. 'This is very unethical
behaviour.'

'To hell with ethics,' she said. 'This is my day
off. I shall do just what I like.'

She deliberately put Aidan's conversation with
Captain Bellingham out of her mind. She would
not confront him with it now. This was what she
wanted. There would be time enough later to
find out what he had said and why. No
arguments today.

They spent the day swimming and sunbathing,
eating fruit, dozing. Aidan bought watermelon
slices from beach vendors and they ate the succu-
lent pink flesh, spitting out the seeds, seeing who
could spit the furthest. They were floating on an
intoxication of laughter and love, sun and sea,
the past forgotten.

'We mustn't forget the time,' said Shelly, lying back, her eyes closed to the dazzling sun. 'The last launch leaves the quay at three-thirty p.m., so we need to be at the bus stop by three p.m.'

'Don't worry. We've plenty of time. We'll start walking back in ten minutes. Race you to the sea for a last swim!'

She was quite reckless now, taking off the top of her bikini as soon as she was in deep water, tucking it into the band of her bikini pants.

'What happens if you lose that top?' Aidan teased. 'It could fall out.'

'I should expect you to do the decent thing and provide me with alternative cover,' said Shelly airily.

'What a ruthless woman,' said Aidan. 'No mercy whatsoever.'

They packed up their few belongings, raked over the sand so that the imprint of their bodies disappeared, and began the long walk back to the beginning of the beach, where the bus would be waiting. Aidan cleaned his glasses and put them back on. Shelly's shoulders were glowing from the warmth of the day and her heart was glowing too. Whatever Aidan had told Captain Bellingham, she did not care. Her work record would take care of that. She had never put a foot wrong. It was gold stars all the way.

They splashed through the sea, not holding hands. They were not lovebirds. But they were easy with each other, with the familiarity of long years of knowing, of a caring that was spilling over into the present.

Ahead was a group of people at the water's edge, clustered, tense, people crying out in another language. Without saying a word, Aidan began to run. Shelly hitched up her sarong and ran after him, her tote bag bumping on her hip.

'Can I help? What's the matter? I'm a doctor,' he called out as he pushed his way through the crowd.

It was a small child, of about three or four. He was not breathing, sprawled face down on the sand, waves washing over him. Aidan fell on to his knees, not wasting time by getting him out of the sea. He cleaned the foam and seaweed out of the boy's mouth and began mouth-to-mouth resuscitation at once.

'Out of the way, please,' said Shelly. 'Give us space. I'm a doctor too. Doctor, *Doktor*, *Doctrice*. . .' She said it in every language she could think of.

The child was not responding. She began a rhythmical chest pressure, timing herself to Aidan's mouth-to-mouth. Please start breathing, she began to say over to herself, watching the colour of the boy's face. His mouth was tinged with blue. His parents were having hysterics, but there was no time to deal with them.

They were both getting soaked, on their knees with the tide racing in, a late-afternoon breeze whipping up crests of white. Aidan was using one arm to support the boy's body and the other to support his head and seal the nose.

'Telefonieren der Krankenwagen,' shouted Shelly urgently, hoping she had got the right words. Her German was schoolgirl standard.

'Shift him,' Shelly said as Aidan came up for air. They both moved the child further up the beach in one co-ordinated movement. Aidan's eyes signalled a swift acknowledgement before he went back to the boy's mouth.

They had to keep working. Fifteen minutes was not too long; it could take longer. How could a day be full of laughter and fun and sunshine and then suddenly the cold hand of disaster strike a happy family? The parents were an ordinary young couple, clinging to each other now with stricken faces. They had to save the life of their son.

Aidan stopped to listen for air leaving the lungs after every four blows, watching the chest wall for movement. They worked closely on the boy, both beginning to tire.

Suddenly the child coughed and choked and threw up a spew of water. They looked at each other with hope. Quickly Aidan turned him over into the recovery position and pumped the water out of his lungs. The boy was gasping, clawing in air to his starved lungs.

'Now we can move him,' he said. They lifted him on to the sand, called for towels to wrap him

to keep him warm, told bystanders to assist the
ambulancemen to find them.

'*Danke, danke*,' said the young mother, wanting
to take the boy in her arms. '*Ich bin tief—*'

'Not yet lady, later. You'll have plenty of time
to cuddle him later,' said Shelly. She sat back on
her heels, exhausted. Aidan was grey-faced. She
saw that the new skin on one of his fingers
had split.

They stayed with the couple till the medics
arrived and the family were transferred to an
ambulance. The beach crowds were thinning as
families trooped back to their apartments.

Then they looked at each other.

'Oh, my God,' said Aidan.

It was nearly four o'clock. The *Clipper Countess*
was due to weigh anchor and sail at four. They
ran to the bus stop. There was no bus. It had
gone long ago. They hailed a cruising taxi, one
of few at the resort, and tried to tell the driver
that they wanted him to take them to the quay,
wasting precious time trying to explain the exact
location of the floating pontoon.

When they got to the deserted quay, there was
no launch waiting. The distinctive shipping-line
umbrella had gone. The iced water urn had gone.
The *Clipper Countess* looked a long way off at
sea. They could hardly swim for it.

'They're going without us,' Shelly gasped.

'They can't,' said Aidan firmly. 'You're the doctor. They check us on and off with those cruise

cards. They must know two people are missing. They must know that one of them is you.'

She wept, her pent-up feelings let loose, tears running down her warm cheeks. 'I'm finished. I'm done for. I've never, ever done anything like this before.'

'Then you'll have to marry me, won't you?' he murmured. Shelly was not sure if that was what Aidan said. It didn't matter. She was too distressed to care what he said. 'To save your reputation. To keep the wolf from the door.'

Then they saw the white speck of a tender leaving the liner, heading towards them, the foam of its wake like a ribbon of forgiveness.

'They've seen us,' she breathed with relief.

Shelly couldn't speak. She held on to Aidan's arm, trying to calm her racing heart. Oh, there were going to be such repercussions. She had to be cool and professional now to save her career. Captain Bellingham would link this with Aidan's warning. Had he used the word unreliable or unstable?

They walked along the floating pontoon, waiting for the launch to reach them. Aidan did not look in the least put out. He was a passenger. He had paid the full fare. He could bluff it out if he had to.

The officer in charge of the launch was enjoying every minute. 'Well, well, well,' he grinned, coming alongside neatly, expecting them to board without the security of the engine cut being off.

'What a turn-up! The whole ship's waiting for you two. Got shipwrecked, did you?'

Shelly was speechless. She climbed aboard and sat silently, clutching her bag.

'Emergency,' said Aidan evenly. 'A child was drowning.'

'Well, I wouldn't be in your shoes, Doctor. The captain's livid. He'll probably cancel all the next shore leave.'

Shelly's heart fell. If she was reprimanded then that was OK, but it was not right if the whole crew suffered. She stared ahead, refusing to look at Aidan. It was not his fault but if she had been alone she would have probably started walking back earlier. No last swim. But then the child might have died without fast medical help. They were there at the right moment. Fate had meant them to be there.

She felt her courage return. They had done the right thing. So what? The ship was going to be twenty minutes late leaving. It could easily make up that time in the night. And she would tell Captain Bellingham that if he got awkward. A child's life was worth more than twenty minutes of a powerful shipping company's time.

The deputy captain was waiting at the entrance to Deck C, his face blank. 'Straight to the captain on the navigational bridge, please, Doctor.'

'You mean like this?' Shelly wrapped the folds of the wet sarong closer round her near-naked body. 'Can't I change into uniform?'

'Straight away and any way,' he smirked. Shelly could have hit him. The righteous so-and-so! Wait till he had a boil in an awkward place.

Captain Bellingham was not in a good mood. He kept her waiting till she was chilled and shivering in the air-conditioning.

'I didn't expect this of you, Doctor Smith,' he said coldly. 'You are one of my best officers. If it had been anyone else I would have sailed without them.'

'And I didn't expect to find a child drowning on the beach,' said Shelly, fighting back. 'And not just drowning, Captain, but near to dying. Four years old, Captain. I believe you have grandchildren of that age. It took fifteen minutes to get him breathing; another ten before the ambulance arrived.'

He didn't expect that answer. He had expected a cowering and repentant female, not this tigress.

'It's one of the first shipboard regulations,' he began again, nettled. 'The ship doesn't wait.'

'And it's my Hippocratic oath, Captain, to save lives. I was not intending to be late; in fact, I was returning to the ship in good time. Was I supposed to say to the parents, Sorry, but I can't stop now? I can't attend to your child. I have to be back on board the British luxury liner *Clipper Countess* before she sails for Madeira, just in case first-sitting dinner might be served late.'

Shelly was seething, so full of anger that she should be reprimanded, aware that she was in the

wrong but that there had been a good reason and
that should be taken into consideration.

'We've waited twenty minutes. We are sailing
twenty minutes late. Sailing times are rigid for
good reasons. Ever heard of tides? It's inexcus-
able, Doctor.'

Aidan was at the entrance to the bridge. How
he had got there, Shelly was never to know. He
stood, filling the doorway with his height, his
bulk, every inch of him exuding authority. He did
not look at Shelly in her creased sarong, her hair
in rats' tails. Instead he looked calmly straight at
the captain.

'But I doubt if the shareholders would have
relished the publicity if the *Clipper Countess* was
held responsible for this little boy's death because
the ship's doctor dared not be late back on ship.'
Aidan took a few steps forward, his hands
clenched. 'The boy's name is Gustav Klingel. He
is almost four and because we stopped to help
he will see his fourth birthday. I think Dr Smith
deserves a commendation, not a dressing down.
And if she doesn't change into something dry
pretty soon she'll catch a chill.'

'I shall have to put in a report,' said the captain.

'And I shall be happy to give any explanation
required,' said Shelly, trying to stay polite.

'Well, you'd better get changed, Doctor. . .'
The captain turned away. The ship was sailing
westerly round the island, passengers hanging
over the rails to watch the barren brown coast

passing by. 'Once clear we'll set a north-northwesterly course towards Madeira.'

'I'll voluntarily stay on board at the next two ports of call,' said Shelly. 'But please don't stop all crew leave. Don't punish everyone.'

She heard Aidan's sharp intake of breath. She knew Funchal was his favourite port, that he was looking forward to it. He'd been talking about seeing Funchal that afternoon.

'It won't be necessary to curtail crew leave,' said the captain drily. 'As you know, we dock in the harbour. You could run back. I will accept your offer in good faith. But I shall still have to make a report.'

'Damn your report,' said Aidan angrily.

CHAPTER SIX

WORD went round the *Clipper Countess* faster than the offer of a free drink that the ship's doctor was a heroine. With each telling the story was embroidered and, by the time it got back to Shelly at the evening surgery, she had apparently swum out to sea to save the boy despite cramp and exhaustion and a powerful current. It was embarrassing.

'What about the sharks?' she said to Jane. 'Hasn't anyone mentioned the sharks? There were at least three of them at the last count.'

'And you had a very handsome colleague, tall, dark and devastating,' said Jane, tidying the treatment-room.

'You know Aidan Trent. You've dressed his burnt hand enough days this trip. I used to work with him at Kingham General, my first hospital. It was purely accidental that we met on the beach,' said Shelly, exasperated, refusing to be drawn. 'Now, would you like to show in the first patient?'

'It's Mrs Scott-Card.'

The bronze-haired woman had gone ethnic and was wearing a silver-embroidered caftan obviously purchased during the Casablanca port of call. She perched herself on the chair and leaned towards

FREE GIFTS!   Play   **FREE BOOKS!**

CASINO JUBILEE

"Scratch'n Match" Game

PEEL OFF LABEL

PLACE LABEL INSIDE

CLAIM UP TO 4 FREE BOOKS, PLUS A FREE NECKLACE

See inside

NO RISK, NO OBLIGATION TO BUY...NOW OR EVER!

CASINO JUBILEE

"Scratch'n Match" Game

Here's how to play:

1. Peel off label from front cover. Place it in the space provided opposite. With a coin carefully scratch away the silver box. This makes you eligible to receive two or more free books, and possibly another gift, depending upon what is revealed beneath the scratch-off area.

2. Send back this card and you'll receive specially selected Love on Call novels. These books have a cover price of £1.99 each, but they are yours to keep absolutely free.

3. There's no catch. You're under no obligation to buy anything. We charge nothing for your first shipment. And you don't have to make any minimum number of purchases - not even one!

4. The fact is thousands of readers enjoy receiving books by mail from the Reader Service, at least a month before they're available in the shops. They like the convenience of home delivery, and there is no extra charge for postage and packing.

5. We hope that after receiving your free books you'll want to remain a subscriber. But the choice is yours - to continue or cancel, anytime at all! So why not take up our invitation, with no risk of any kind. You'll be glad you did!

*Prices subject to change without notice.

YOURS FREE!

You'll look like a million dollars when you wear this elegant necklace! It's cobra link chain is a generous 18" long and its lustrous simulated pearl is mounted in an attractive pendant.

(Pictured larger to show di

CASINO JUBILEE
"Scratch'n Match" Game

SCRATCH HERE ?

CHECK CLAIM CHART BELOW
FOR YOUR FREE GIFTS!

2A6D

YES! I have placed my label from the front cover in the space provided above and scratched away the silver box. Please send me all the gifts for which I qualify. I understand that I am under no obligation to purchase any books, as explained on the back and on the opposite page. I am over 18 years of age.

BLOCK CAPITALS PLEASE

MS/MRS/MISS/MR _____

ADDRESS _____

_____ POSTCODE _____

CASINO JUBILEE CLAIM CHART				
🍒	🍒	🍒	WORTH 4 FREE BOOKS A FREE NECKLACE AND MYSTERY GIFT	
🍒	🔔	🍒	WORTH 4 FREE BOOKS	
🔔	🔔	🍒	WORTH 3 FREE BOOKS	CLAIM Nº 1,528

Mills & Boon Reader Service

FREEPOST

Croydon
Surrey
CR9 3WZ

NO
STAMP
NEEDED

Shelly, all lash-building mascara and eyebrow pencil.

'Are you well enough to be taking surgery?' she asked anxiously. 'It must have been awful and you must be exhausted. That poor little boy. We're all so proud of you, Doctor. We think you ought to get an award.'

'Heavens, no,' said Shelly, getting out Mrs Scott-Card's notes. 'I happened to be there at the right time and used a normal medical procedure. Now, what can I do for you? How's your indigestion? Do you need some more tablets?'

'And who was this gorgeous man with you? I saw you coming aboard together. Have you been holding out on us?'

Shelly took a deep breath. Mrs Scott-Card did not mean to be obnoxious. She had way more than average curiosity and that, combined with a thick skin, made her impossible. 'If you go up to the Ensign bar before dinner you'll be able to buy him a hero's drink. That's where he can usually be found. He's one of the passengers,' said Shelly.

'Oh, how thrilling,' Mrs Scott-Card trilled. 'I'll do just that. I'd love to talk to him. He looks such an interesting man.' She got up with a swish of skirt, about to sweep out.

'Don't you want to see me about something?'

'I'm feeling much better already.' She smiled brightly. 'It must be your healing presence. We shall have to start calling you St Shelly.'

'Watch my halo,' said Shelly. 'Tell me if it slips.'

Evening surgery turned into a third-degree marathon, though, as expected, she doled out pints of calamine lotion and zinc ointment. Several men had exposed their white-skinned torsos for the first time that summer and had severe sunburn with blistering. Two young brothers had heat exhaustion and she admitted them to a ward together for tepid sponging and to check their fluid balance, giving fluids to replace the loss of salt.

'They'll be as right as rain in no time,' she told their mother. 'You'll have them back as soon as the fever has gone. We'd like to keep an eye on them.'

'We thought we were so careful,' the mother wailed.

'The midday temperature today was surprisingly high, especially on the beach. Don't worry, they are going to be all right,' Shelly reassured her.

Shelly left the boys in the good care of Jane, ordering juice and ice cream from the dining-room for their supper in case they felt hungry. There were two members of the crew in the crew ward, both complaining of headaches and aches and pains. She had thought it best to isolate them, as influenza was an acutely infectious disease. It was caused by a germ breathed in through the nose or mouth and could fly round a small group living almost on top of each other.

'I'm afraid you're going to have to stay here

for a couple of days until your temperatures fall,' said Shelly. 'I don't want an epidemic on my hands. I'll prescribe paracetamol every four hours to make you feel more comfortable.'

'Can we have the telly on, Doctor?'

'Of course. All mod cons. There's even remote control. But keep the volume down, please, or Sister will turn it off. Please remember you aren't the only patients in the medical centre tonight.'

It was a cooler evening with a strong wind and choppy seas as the *Clipper Countess* headed for the island of Madeira. Shelly took a walk along the decks, head against the wind, her shirt flapping. It was invigorating and cleansing. She saw a familiar figure in the distance.

'How could you, Shelly? You've been sending everyone to me in the bar! Quite ruined my evening.' Aidan was striding towards her, none too pleased. 'If I'd drunk every drink I've been offered tonight I'd be rolling by now, not walking.'

'My hero,' Shelly murmured, trying to pass him.

'I suppose it was your idea of a joke,' he fumed, his lips set. He stood squarely in front of her.

'I'm sure you loved every minute of it. All that genuine adulation.' Shelly smiled, knowing she had found his vulnerable spot. He hated any fuss.

'You did it on purpose, witch. I shall never get rid of some of those women. They'll plague me for the rest of the cruise, wanting to buy me drinks.' But his distress was not really heart-deep.

Shelly was sure she could detect a twitch of amusement touching his sardonic features.

'I'm sure Elaine will cope with any harem that might start ambushing you. That reticent woman is hiding a vein of inner steel,' said Shelly lightly. She tried to pass him again but he caught hold of her arm, pulling her back.

'What makes you say that?'

'She clings to you firmly enough.'

'So that's it,' said Aidan, shaking his head incredulously. 'My God, it's all about Elaine. You're jealous, Shelly. Well, that's priceless and I've never heard anything so ridiculous. Elaine is just someone I've met on the ship. She means nothing to me.'

'That's all right, then. She'll be able to protect you from any unwanted advances. I'm surprised she wasn't with you in the bar.' Shelly felt the conversation was getting out of control. Why had she mentioned Elaine? She had no wish to discuss her.

'No, it's not all right. And I don't like the way you're talking about her. Elaine doesn't drink. You ought to know that; she's on your table at second sitting.'

His voice was a mixture of affection and contempt. Shelly knew she had gone too far. Perhaps he did feel some affection for this Elaine. Shipboard romances were nothing new and happened every cruise. Starlit decks were a powerful aphrodisiac. There was always some woman weeping on the dockside at Southampton as the passengers parted at the end of the cruise.

'She doesn't gamble either,' Aidan went on. 'So are you coming to the casino night this evening? It's all for a good cause. Ship's charities.'

'What a paragon. Elaine should be wearing the halo, not me,' said Shelly, surprised at the strength of her feelings. As Aidan said, it was ridiculous. Aidan meant nothing to her now and she should be glad that he was enjoying the company of the little shrimp.

'But don't come if you are still in this same vile mood,' said Aidan abruptly, catching her arm and turning her to face him. 'But if your normal good humour returns then I'd be happy to buy you today's cocktail and help you lose a lot of money on the tables.'

'I don't need any help,' said Shelly. 'I always lose.'

It was curious how she had such a feeling of attachment and of belonging to this man. The bonds were not yet fully severed. Perhaps they never had. She needed open-heart surgery.

'See you at the casino some time after ten.'

After dinner Shelly checked on her patients. The two boys were asleep, but still flushed. The crewmen were playing cards, obviously feeling better. Shelly was relieved. The last thing she wanted was a flu epidemic.

Casino night. She did not want to go, yet part of her longed to be with Aidan. The truce had worked perfectly all day on the beach. Could it survive the evening as well?

She showered, letting the lukewarm water run over her body. She examined her skin but there were no unwanted strap marks or sunburn. Her sunbathing had been well monitored and her body was a glowing honey tan, apart from the white triangle and line on her hips covered by her bikini pants.

The choice was hers. An early night with a good book and a pot of tea, or a late night of unrestrained and wild-eyed gambling at the tables? Shelly thought of the pile of good books she had read in the last three years and went to her wardrobe. She had one really stunning outfit bought in a moment of reckless spending. Tonight seemed the right night to wear it.

Aidan caught his breath as he saw Shelly coming into the casino-night lounge. She looked beautiful. The day's sun and relaxation had brought a glow to her cheeks; her long brown hair hung like silk. Her body was swathed in layers of nearly black chiffon, so light and airy, the skirt swirling round her ankles, the hem ruffled, a shimmer in the material that brought glamour into every step. The dress was unstructured and utterly feminine.

Aidan came over to her and brought her hand to his lips. 'You look wonderful,' he said simply.

'Thank you.' She smiled at him. 'Is our truce still on? Will it last out the evening?'

'Of course. I wouldn't have it any other way.'

He led her to the bar and called over the barman. 'An Amaretto Rose for this beautiful woman,' he said.

Shelly hid her smile. The barman was grinning too. He was not used to seeing quite so much of the ship's doctor. The bare shoulders and shoestring straps were very unmedical and extremely revealing.

'And just what is an Amaretto Rose?' Shelly asked happily, making herself comfortable on a bar stool. She would have drunk cold tea. 'It sounds a bit horticultural.'

'It's to celebrate our imminent arrival at Madeira. There are strawberries, lemon, lime and cream. . .with some glorious almond liqueur to give it some zip,' said Aidan, taking her hand. 'Do you like the sound of that?'

She liked the sound of his voice. He was in the mood for talking and she encouraged him, asking questions that led him on. She wanted to know everything that had happened to him in the last three years. Work and more work, it seemed; several conferences, a couple of intense courses on the new laser-surgery techniques. He said nothing about his private life. And why should he? She had walked out on him. Perhaps there had been no private life. Aidan was that kind of man.

He moved a pile of green plastic discs along the bar towards her and grinned, his eyes deliberately

glinting behind his glasses. 'There you are.
You can lose those on the tables. Let's go
circulate.'

Shelly cruised the tables, drink in hand. She
felt quite decadent. There were all sorts of games,
some that could not be classed as gambling at all.
As well as the usual blackjack and roulette, there
were some innocent garden-fête-type games—
guess which thimble had the walnut under it and
race a horse along a course according to the deal-
ing of the cards.

'Hearts. You move four paces!' Terribly exciting. Shelly won another green disc for coming first
with her horse, a heart card. But her pile of discs
was slowly going down. She was useless at roulette
and didn't really understand the skill required for
blackjack.

Shelly won a bottle of suntan lotion and a pair
of bright green sunglasses on the tombola. She
gave the sunglasses to a little girl who should have
been in bed.

'Having fun?' Aidan brushed past her. He had
a handful of discs. 'I keep winning,' he said
absently. 'I'm on a winning streak. Perhaps you
ought to come with me. I don't win when I'm
with you. Then I'm a loser.'

The double-edged words cut hard. More things
were being said than voiced. He was standing so
close that Shelly ceased to know where she ended
and he began. She stared at the slope of his shoulders, longing to put her hands on them, to touch

the solid wall of his chest, to say to him, Let's go somewhere quiet.

Shelly's glance kept straying towards Aidan. She never tired of his splendid looks, wondered if every other woman in the room thought he was as gorgeous. The ship's newspaper said that Jupiter was colliding with somewhere that day. Shelly reckoned the planet must be colliding with her. It had been an unforgettable and disturbing a day. And it wasn't nearly finished yet.

Aidan took her elbow and steered her away from the casino. 'Cleaned out,' he said casually. 'Do you fancy a drink? Tea or coffee? I think you've had enough of those Amaretto Roses. One bonus of giving up smoking is that my sense of smell is really acute and I can smell that almond liqueur on your breath. It's heavenly.'

He could also smell the sweet scent of her skin and it was driving him crazy. He wanted to spirit her away to some safe and secret haven and kiss her till she gave in to him and all that silky skin was wrapped around him.

They went on deck and leaned on the rail. A crewman was hosing it down and they sidestepped the wet patches, Shelly scooping up an armful of filmy skirt out of the way. Her Frank Usher dress had cost a lot of money and she loved wearing it. It gave her a special kind of confidence, to know that she was looking good. And hadn't Aidan said that?

She stared down at the froth of white wash, a

cascade of unfinished lace or lace with mistakes in it. The blue sea was not blue at all but a glossy navy with tinges of black in the swells. There were mountains under that sea and Shelly could believe their existence, smell long-decayed flowers, the bones of untroubled animals, sleeping their ancient sleep.

'The truce has worked well today,' said Aidan evenly. He was standing close with the sleeve of his jacket brushing her skin, staring out to sea.

'Yes, it's worked fine, said Shelly. 'Let's keep it that way.' She did not mention his conversation with the captain, though she was anxious to know what he had said. It could only fuel the antagonism between them and first she needed to know how to deal with his action. It wouldn't be easy.

'Are you ready yet to tell me why you left me?'

It came out of the blue. His intense eyes were burning into her, the lenses magnifying the light. Shelly swallowed her dismay and floundered for words.

'Aidan, I will try to explain some of the reasons,' she said slowly. 'But don't push me. I can't tell you all of it at once. Everything between us was fine, believe me. I was very happy and I thought it would go on forever. . .'

'So did I,' said Aidan coldly. 'It was one of those perfect love affairs. The kind you only dream about.'

'But then something happened to me. . . .a sort of health problem. . .that I couldn't share. And you weren't there.'

'You couldn't share a health problem?' He looked at her incredulously. 'Shelly, we're both doctors. Are you seriously trying to tell me that you had an illness, a disease, that you weren't able to tell me about? What was it?' Suddenly he got her by the shoulders and shook her fiercely. 'Was it cancer?'

'Let me go, Aidan. Don't be so rough.' Shelly shook her head. 'No, not that kind of health problem, I'm thankful to say. Not cancer.'

He let her go reluctantly. 'Thank God for that. Well, what other kind is there?' He went very quiet, thinking. 'Are you trying to say that you had a mental illness, a breakdown of some kind? Don't you realise that I could have coped with that? Anything—ingrowing toenails, gout, galloping ecthyma plus rampant eczema. I'd have looked after you, nursed you, sent you to the finest consultants in the country.'

'It was nothing like that,' said Shelly, longing to tell him the whole story. But she dared not. 'It was something happening to me, personally, and I had to go away and deal with it myself. Then. . .' She broke off, the pain of the miscarriage surging back. 'As it happened, it resolved itself.'

'You're talking in riddles,' he said, exasperated, clutching the rail. 'I don't understand a word.

You obviously met another man. That's all I can think of.'

'No, it wasn't another man.' She wanted to say that there would never be any other man for her, but the words stuck in her throat. Just as the word 'baby' stuck in her throat.

'I'm glad about that.'

'You believe me?'

'I don't think you've ever knowingly lied to me. You've always been honest with me even if I haven't a clue what you're talking about. I thought it was another man or something that I had done. You're a very complicated woman.'

How could she tell him that it was something he had done, something they had created together? That partly it had been her fault, forgetting to take the Pill after night duty? Another smile touched her face and Aidan could stand it no longer. He was behind her, his arms closing round her, drawing her close. She felt his face against her ear, his glasses tangling with her hair.

'I thought I had stopped loving you,' he murmured. 'But I haven't. I don't care if you've been to prison, done time, killed a patient, had to flee the country because the fraud squad were after you. In other words. . .the fires of love have never cooled, my darling.'

Shelly laughed and it was a delicious sound as she felt the warmth of his body close to her back. 'Oh, Aidan, now you're not being sensible. We're just friends, fairly loving friends, if you like.'

'Friends? Well, yes, I'll go for that. . .but loving friends is much better. Do loving friends make love?' He turned her round swiftly and his mouth crushed her lips before she could answer, fastening her to him. The ecstatic sensation unleashed a spring that was coiled inside her. But she tried to restrain his urgency, trying to retain just enough sanity to contain their mutual pleasure.

But the coolness of the night breeze did nothing to dampen the tumult of their emotions. Shelly felt the swollen curves of her breasts feasting on the hardness of his body. She wanted more of his tenderness. She'd been three years in the wilderness and her body was exploding with desire. Their lovemaking had always had a special intimacy and she was greedy to taste it again.

'Shelly. . .?' he asked huskily, breaking away.

'I think we are providing the late-night cabaret,' she murmured, looking past his shoulder.

There were other couples taking the night air, strolling at a discreet distance, but obviously intrigued by the loving embrace.

'Damn it. I can't stand an audience. Let's go inside.'

'It's very late. I have to get some sleep.'

'Of course. I'll walk you to your cabin.' He clasped her hand in a normal, casual way. It was as if they had never been parted.

They went down the mirrored stairs, going the wrong way without thinking and having to walk through the empty dining-room, already laid for breakfast. Shelly didn't care how long it took to reach her cabin. Hours would do. She looked up at him, loving every curve of his body, those broad sloping shoulders, the shape of his dark head, the remoteness of his steadfast look ahead. Yet he was still holding her hand, making a tangible link between them. He could not be that remote from her even if his thoughts were elsewhere.

They stopped outside the medical centre. Shelly felt her professional cloak slipping over her shoulders. She had patients to look after.

'I know. You want to look at your patients,' said Aidan. 'I'll come with you. Valuable second opinion,' he added lightly.

But they were all soundly asleep. Even the steward on duty was dozing.

'Bless 'em,' said Aidan paternally.

He took her key from her hand and opened the door to her cabin. 'Don't send me away,' he said, standing so tall in the half-light, the interior of her cabin familiar and reassuring.

She was surprised at her own tumultuous feelings. She drew in a long, ragged breath; everything seemed to be slowing down and unstructured. This man was like a magnet. She could not say no to him. She wanted him, to forget all the hurt of the last three years in his embrace. Her body was crying out to be held and loved.

There was only one small light on, the one she always left on over her desk. The pool of light

did not reach the bed. Her steward had turned
the covers down, the triangle of white sheet and
smooth pillow the envelope of an invitation.

Aidan was exploring her dress, running
his hands over her body. 'How do we get this
beautiful thing off without ruining it?'

She guided his hands and the dress slipped over
her head like gossamer wings. She stood quite
still in her dark lacy bra and pants, not daring to
move. It seemed he could never have enough of
touching her, stroking her skin, wondering at her
softness and feminine curves.

'Shelly, Shelly, I've missed you so much,' he
whispered huskily. 'I thought I was going out of
my mind. Never thought I would find you here.
Let me love you. That's all I ask. Then I'll stay
out of your life and you need never see me again.'

He didn't wait for an answer but lifted her in
his arms and carried her over to the bed. The
warm, fragrant air was full of love and caring.
There was no way she could shatter it with a loud
protest or unseemly struggle. But struggling was
a long way from her mind. Her arms curved round
him, loving the soft feel of his hair curling into
the nape of his neck.

He took off his glasses and put them beside her
bed. Then he was wrenching at his shirt as if he
had forgotten how buttons fastened. Shelly had
to smile at his ineptness. Her fingers skimmed
down the buttons, eager for the first sight and the
first touch of that dark hair on his chest. She

sighed deeply as she breathed in the scent of his
skin and laid her cheek against his pulsing heart.

The muscles shivered along her spine. His shirt
pooled on the floor, somewhere alongside her
dress. In moments they were locked in heated
delight, his mouth intimately exploring hers, his
hands gliding over her silken flesh. His thumb
brushed against her nipples and she arched her
back, glorying in the unbearable ache, moving
against his hand, longing for him to take her
nipples in his mouth.

He slipped the straps of her bra off her shoulders and drew in his breath as he saw the soft
mounds of her breasts. They were so beautiful.
He could never tire of seeing them. He buried
his face into them and the valley between, inhaling
their fragrance, taking a fierce pleasure from the
sensation of their erotic rising buds.

Shelly gave a husky sob of delight as his mouth
fastened on her nipple and his tongue caressed
and enticed her to move with him. Why had she
ever left all this wonderful loving behind. . .?
Why hadn't she trusted his love and let the world
right itself?

His face was smooth in the dim light, like a
young man's; the years had fled with his glasses.
She loved every plane, traced each beloved fea-
ture, bit the firm chin gently with her teeth.
Jupiter colliding with Mars? The planets were certainly colliding in this small cabin.

She could feel Aidan's throbbing male response

and turned to welcome him into the warm and secret cavern of her body.

'Aidan,' she breathed. 'Love me. . .'

CHAPTER SEVEN

'DOCTOR, I'm terribly sorry to wake you up but I think Mr Harris has had a heart attack.' It was Jane's voice, anxious and apologetic, on the telephone.

'Don't you mean Mrs Harris?' said Shelly, surfacing through layers of sleep, fragments of a dream falling from her mind like confetti. She got out of bed and began pulling on a track suit. It was nearly six a.m. and there would be the early birds about. 'She's being treated for angina.'

'No, this is her husband and it does seem quite serious. He's in a bad way.'

Shelly raced to their cabin. The wife and now the husband. . .it did seem very strange. Had they been keeping something from her? Passengers often lied about their medical condition because they wanted to come on a cruise so much. They were afraid that they might be told they were at risk and better off staying at home.

One look at Mr Harris and Shelly knew that it was very serious. He was bending forward with a hand pressed to his chest, restlessly trying to find a more comfortable position. He was very short of breath and his skin was grey with a blue tinge, cold and covered in sweat. He had been sick and was in a near state of collapse.

Shelly didn't need to waste his breath asking questions. She prepared an immediate injection of morphine 15 mg with cyclizine 50 mg and injected it intramuscularly. This would control the pain and give him some relief.

'You can have another injection in three to four hours, when we see how the pain is,' she said soothingly. 'Sister will try and make you more comfortable before we move you down to the medical centre. I'm afraid you need more care than we can give you in your cabin. We need to monitor your temperature, pulse and respiration every hour. Try not to worry, Mr Harris.'

Shelly turned to Gwen Harris, who was watching her husband anxiously, wringing her hands.

'This isn't just angina, like me?' she asked.

'No, Mrs Harris. This is far more serious and your husband needs a lot of care and medical supervision before he gets better. I believe he should be in hospital. I think I should make arrangements to have him flown home by Medivac.'

'Oh, no!' Gwen Harris's hands flew to her mouth.

'Do you know what brought this on, Mrs Harris? Had you been on the dance floor jiving again half the night?'

'Oh, no, we've both been taking it very carefully since the other night. But my husband does

have a very quick temper and we had been arguing,' she admitted.

'Not about postcards, I hope,' said Shelly
calmly.

'No, it was about tomorrow's excursions. We
couldn't agree about which one to go on. He was
determined to go on one that I didn't like the
sound of at all. It was very silly.'

'Yes,' said Shelly. 'You should have decided to
go your separate ways. The marriage vows don't
say you have to do everything together. Now it
looks as if you won't be going ashore at Madeira.
You'll be flying home, I'm afraid.'

Mrs Harris began to weep and Shelly was sorry
that she had used such harsh words. It annoyed
her how daft some people were but it looked as
if arguing was the only spice left in this marriage.
Now they had something really serious to
worry about.

'Medivac are very good,' said Shelly. 'They'll
fly out from the UK in the morning and be able
to pick you up some time after lunch. That'll give
you plenty of time to pack and I'll arrange for a
steward to come and help you. There's some tea
coming along and the steward will give you your
breakfast in bed. You need to take it easy yourself
and try not to worry. I don't want you to become
another patient. Your husband is going to need
all your support.'

A wheelchair had arrived to transport Mr
Harris down to the medical centre. Shelly knew

passengers always preferred a wheelchair if possible. Lying on a stretcher was so humiliating in front of their friends and the crew.

Captain Bellingham had said nothing to Shelly about any shore leave but now it was out of the question. She would have to stay with the Harrises and escort them to the plane. It meant arranging for an ambulance to be at the quayside to take them to the airport and seeing them safely transferred. The airport was about all she would see of Madeira on this visit.

Shelly sighed. It was such a lovely island, one of her favourites, and she had been harbouring a little hope that Aidan might walk around the port with her. She would have loved to take him up the steep, twisting road to the glorious botanical gardens high above Funchal or to have strolled round the ancient fortress of St Lorenzo on the front, where the guards were on duty in their operatic uniforms and plumed hats.

The *Clipper Countess* docked early along the harbour quayside and a local launch bobbed on the water, ready to take passengers across to the harbour steps, a five-minute journey, saving them the half-hour walk round the quay.

Shelly had a busy surgery. Four more crewmen turned up with flu-like symptoms. She was not at all happy about them. The two brothers with heat exhaustion had gone back to their parents. Mr Harris was very poorly. Gwen Harris sat at his side, counting the minutes for the Medivac plane to arrive. She couldn't wait to return to England now.

'I hope he makes it home,' said Jane in an aside to Shelly. 'The pulse rate is less than sixty per minute now. I've raised his legs.'

'I'll come in and give him 1 mg of atropine right away,' said Shelly. 'I've a very odd case with me at the moment. A woman with a mouth that is too dry to eat, I don't know what to make of it; most extraordinary.'

Shelly checked on Mr Harris's condition. She hoped his heart wouldn't stop beating on the way to the plane. The stress of transportation was sometimes too much for a patient. She'd take the compression equipment along with them just in case.

'I'm sorry about that,' said Shelly, returning to the surgery. 'Now explain that all to me again, please.'

Grace Goldsmith took a deep breath. 'My mouth is so dry I can't eat anything. I can only drink and drink but even that doesn't seem to be enough.' Her voice was hoarse, her skin looked dry and there were shadows and unhealthy bags under her eyes. She obviously wasn't sleeping well.

'How about your senses of taste and smell?'

'I've forgotten what anything tastes like. Smell has gone too. . . When I see all the lovely food in the dining-room I could weep. Especially when I've paid for it.'

'How long have you been like this?' Shelly asked curiously. She had no notes on Grace Goldsmith. She had come aboard with a clean bill of health.

The woman began to look distressed and Shelly poured her a glass of water from her vacuum flask. She drank eagerly but even swallowing seemed painful.

'I don't know. . .some months. . .maybe longer.' She shrugged and looked everywhere but at Shelly.

'Haven't you been to your own doctor?'

'I didn't like to. It all seems so silly. He'd say it was all in my imagination. But I thought today would be a good time to see you. . .I don't want to go ashore. I just want to rest somewhere. I've no energy.'

'I'm not surprised. Let me have a look inside your mouth. Open, please,' said Shelly.

There was no saliva in the mouth and the salivary glands were swollen. The tongue was coated. Her eyes were inflamed too, looking sore and gritty.

'You really must see your doctor when you get home. It isn't silly at all. I can give you tear and saliva substitutes for the eyes and mouth; use them three times a day. My nurse will show you how to use them. I also think your general health is poor. You must drink a lot of fruit juice and milky drinks and I'll get the chef to prepare a special diet for you; everything should be very moist and easy to swallow. But the most important thing is to get the right help when you get home.'

Grace Goldsmith began to cry. 'I didn't think anyone would take me seriously. You've been so kind, Doctor. You haven't laughed. I've almost stopped going to meals; so embarrassing, choking on food and having to leave the table. . .'

'No more of that,' said Shelly firmly. 'Take your breakfast and lunch at the pool buffet and your special meals will be ready for you there—lots of nourishing soups and fruit purées, creamy things with delicious sauces. Heavens, I'm making myself feel quite hungry. I might even join you for lunch.'

'Would you do that?' Grace latched on to the offer immediately, though it had only been a joke. 'I'd feel less conspicuous. Just till I get used to asking for it.'

'I will if I can,' Shelly promised with a smile, 'but it may not be possible. I do have a seriously ill patient in one of the wards. See the nurse now, then get yourself a cup of hot chocolate and later on, when the steward comes round with the ice cream, see if you can swallow a little.'

When Shelly eventually found a moment to go on deck she saw that the passengers were queueing up for the launch taking them across the harbour to the steps. Funchal clung to the hills weaving a canopy of flowers and flowering trees, the scent wafting across the water. It was a pretty place yet she remembered when it had not been so picturesque, when every wall had been daubed with political slogans and litter blew along every gutter. The authorities had realised this was driving away tourists and a determined clean-up operation had turned Madeira into one of the Atlantic's most attractive islands.

Then she saw him. She could recognise his tallness and dark, shapely head anywhere. It made her feel sick to see Aidan walking easily down the steep gangway, giving a helping hand to Elaine, who couldn't quite manage the ascent on her own.

He must have felt her eyes on him, for he looked up, searching the decks. Then he saw her, paused as if sending her a special message, and raised his hand briefly in salute.

She waved, just as briefly, and took in a deep breath of contentment. Seeing him was enough, that long moment of eye contact, knowing that everything was all right between them.

Aidan and Elaine joined the queue to get on the launch. Shelly turned away. She'd had enough of watching them.

Moving Mr and Mrs Harris would be done very discreetly when all the passengers going ashore had gone. It was always a distressing manoeuvre and the fewer people about the better. Flying anyone home was kept very quiet because rumours could spread round the ship. In no time it would be an epidemic of legionnaires' disease.

Shelly went back to her cabin. Her steward

followed her with fresh coffee and some croissants. He knew she had not had time for breakfast.

'You're wonderful.' She smiled. 'What would I do without you? Thanks, Dino.'

She showered quickly and put on a fresh uniform. No jeans and T-shirt for this visit to Funchal. She twisted her hair up into a knot.

There was no time to have lunch with Grace Goldsmith but Shelly made a flying check to the lido deck and found the woman sitting by herself in the shade of a sun parasol near the pool, slowly spooning a bowl of liquidised beef and vegetable soup.

'And for afters I've got puréed apricots and cream. So I'll see how I get on with that,' said Grace. She toasted Shelly with a sip from a glass of orange juice. 'Thank you, Doctor. I can't tell you what a relief it was to talk to you. I thought I was going mad.'

Shelly felt a sudden constriction of her own throat. She knew the feeling, as if the world had withdrawn its support. She had felt like that when she had left Aidan. As if she was going mad on her own, as if she could not think straight.

'Come and see me again,' said Shelly. 'We'll talk some more. It all helps.'

The woman was near to tears again, so Shelly left quickly. Grace needed building up, mentally and physically. It couldn't be done in the few days left of the cruise but the foundation could be laid.

The ambulance had arrived. It was parked near a lower gangway so that Mr Harris could be carried off more easily. Everything was organised to the last minute, like a royal event. Their luggage would be loaded first, then Mrs Harris, then the patient. Shelly stood on the quayside enjoying the sunshine, wondering if she would have time when she got back to buy her mother a pretty tablecloth. The stalls of embroidered goods were laid out in orderly lines, ready to catch the returning passengers wanting to spend the last of their currency.

'This is all made by my daughter,' said a stall-holder expansively, sensing Shelly's interest in the array of embroidery and drawn threadwork.

'She certainly has been very busy,' said Shelly.

She couldn't shop because suddenly her mouth had gone dry. Aidan was coming towards her along the quay. He'd come off a returning launch. There was no Elaine clinging to his arm. He looked purposeful, the man she had known so well striding the wards at Kingham's. He came and stood beside her.

'Heard you might have a transport problem,' he said, his eyes boring into her. 'Can I come along with you?'

'Who told you?'

'I have my contacts.'

Jane or Frances, Shelly guessed. He'd had a check in surgery recently. There was a small dressing on his split finger.

'Thank you,' she said, her voice lost somewhere in her emotion. 'That would be very helpful. I might need you. Elaine not with you?'

'I believe she's gone shopping.' He sounded completely uninterested. But he was interested in the Harrises.

She introduced Aidan to Mrs Harris and knew that having a London consultant with them would help calm the woman's fears.

'May I?' Aidan looked towards the patient for permission. 'Do you mind?'

'Please do. A second opinion would be great.'

Aidan's professional manner was marvellous. He had a reassuring way of talking to patients, of giving them his full attention. Shelly could see Mrs Harris relaxing as he listened to her, adding his own comments.

The journey to the Santa Cruz airport was nineteen kilometres from Funchal and Shelly had a very sick patient to look after in the jolting ambulance; many of the roads in Funchal were cobbled. Aidan was a godsend. She could not be grateful enough. He knew exactly what to do. Somehow there seemed to be telepathy between them. Neither spoke of their night of lovemaking, but the residual glow was there, like a warm web of bonding, something that could not be destroyed by the day's events. Her body was relaxed, her skin smooth and a smile hovered near her mouth.

It was a day of moderate temperature, perfect sunshine with a cooling breeze that would have made sightseeing a pleasure. Flowers in abundance hung from balconies and lamps, creating a haze of blue jacaranda. Flower sellers in their national costume sat on every corner with huge wickerwork baskets of lilies. Landscaped gardens were full of flowering trees and plants with running water and ponds with nonchalant ducks. Orchids grew wild and abundantly.

'You are very efficient,' he murmured to her. 'If I ever have another accident, will you please make sure you are available?'

'You never told me exactly what happened,' she said lightly. 'You said you would.'

'Didn't I?' He knew perfectly well that he hadn't. 'There's not much to tell.'

'I don't believe you, Aidan,' said Shelly. 'Your injuries were not consistent with putting out a fire. I'm sure you're keeping something from me.'

'You haven't exactly been open with me either,' he said dangerously. 'Perhaps it's time for some frank talking from both of us. Madeira could be the right time and the right place, an island of sugar and wine and bananas. What could be more pleasant? Shelly, I've waited long enough. Can't we both stop playing games?'

Nothing had prepared her for the sweet persuasion of his voice and the faint veil of affection in his gaze. She recognised the need for honesty now. She wanted to tell him but was afraid of what she might see come into his eyes, the scorn, the derision, the anger.

The rattling ambulance noisily prevented her from having to make a reply. She smoothed her hair with a disturbed, fluttering gesture. 'Ah, we're approaching the airport at Santa Cruz. Mr Harris has endured the journey well—the thought of going home has been like a tonic. Nearly there, Mr Harris,' she said to her patient. 'Not long now.'

'I'll be all right once I get home,' he said with a weak smile at his wife.

'That's right, love. We'll be home in a couple of hours,' said Gwen Harris, holding his hand.

The Medivac plane was parked discreetly away from the commercial passenger air terminal. The accompanying doctor and nurse were waiting by the plane and greeted Shelly in a friendly way. She had worked with them before. Shelly introduced Aidan, then handed over Mr Harris's notes. She also mentioned Mrs Harris's angina.

'OK, let's get Mr Harris on board. We've been given a take-off slot and we don't want to miss it.'

The transfer went smoothly and Shelly was relieved when Mr Harris was safely aboard the plane. A burden rolled off her shoulders. She had seven hundred other passengers to look after and she wanted to get back to doing that.

'We'll get a taxi back to the ship,' said Aidan to the Portuguese ambulance driver. 'But thanks for bringing us out here.'

Shelly didn't argue; the ambulance could return

the medical centre's equipment. She wanted to be alone with Aidan. She could never have enough of touching him, or being near him, of listening to his voice. It was like an addiction.

'With no cure,' she said to herself.

'We'll stop in Funchal for some well-deserved coffee,' said Aidan. 'We could both do with a drink after that journey. I had my fingers crossed the whole time.'

'We all hate losing a patient but it's even worse on board ship. Even though we try to keep it quiet, somehow the other passengers always seem to find out. Then it casts a sort of gloom and the entertainments people have a hard time trying to lift it and getting things back to normal.'

'Don't worry, Shelly, I think Mr Harris will make it. Thanks to your good care. You acted very swiftly getting Medivac out here. If you had dithered for twenty-four hours it might have been a different story.'

The taxi dropped them in the town centre, near the dark red stone of the cathedral. Shelly felt as if she was playing truant and that she ought to go straight back to the ship.

'Nobody said you had to return to the ship immediately,' said Aidan, reading her mind. 'Surely you deserve a coffee and a few moments of rest and relaxation? It must have been a stressful day. As your doctor, I prescribe a seat in the sun and a gentle stroll back to the ship.'

'But you're not my doctor.'

'Well, I ought to be. I've just appointed myself,' he grinned down at her.

Shelly did not know what to make of that remark. But she let it go, preferring to keep everything light.

He guided her towards an open-air café in the Rue J Tavira. The tables on the pavement were laid with blue cloths and carnations in vases, and at the end of the road was the sparkling blue sea and more flowering trees. It was an idyllic place. Be it ten minutes or twenty minutes, Shelly was determined to enjoy these precious moments with Aidan.

He ordered coffee Americano and some honey pastries.

'I don't suppose you had any lunch.'

'Much too busy. Morning surgery went on late as well. I had a most unusual case.' Shelly described Grace Goldsmith's symptoms without mentioning her name. Aidan listened intently.

'That sound like Sjögren's syndrome,' he said, surprisingly. 'It can lead to a lot of ill-health. Any sign of arthritis?'

'Sjögren's syndrome? I never thought to ask about arthritis,' said Shelly, stricken. 'Is it connected?'

He nodded. 'There are several painless tests available, most of which are non-invasive and easily carried out. There's excellent treatment nowadays. I'll give you the address of the BSSA in the UK which you can give to this lady. They have produced an advisory guide which your patient and her doctor might find helpful.'

Shelly could not stop herself. She put her hands over his hands, aware of the difference in skin texture. She ran her thumb gently over his palms, feeling the scarring on one, the smoothness of the other.

'Last night was wonderful,' she said after a long pause.

'I thought you were never going to mention it,' he teased gently. 'You're too modest, my darling. It was glorious.'

It was not easy to talk about it. Shelly averted her gaze.

An old woman was taking her time crossing the road behind them. She was slow and stumbling, wrapped in dark clothes, her mind in another world. Shelly and Aidan smiled at each other as a taxi stopped in the middle of the road and the driver leaned over and opened the door for the old woman to get in.

'Perhaps she's his mother.'

'Or perhaps she's a well-known local road hazard with no memory of where she lives.' Shelly smiled, sipping her coffee. 'So, Aidan, tell me. What actually happened to your hand?'

'Not a lot to tell. It was the usual sort of barbecue, chops and hamburgers and sausages. My sister couldn't get the heat going and they weren't cooking fast enough. She was getting impatient and some idiot threw on methylated spirits to get

it going.' He paused, not willing to go on. It was
like diving back into an unpleasant dream.

'Surely you didn't try to rescue a sausage?' said
Shelly lightly, prompting him on.

'No, it was my nephew, Jamie. He's only four.
He stumbled in his haste to reach his mother as
the sheet of flame shot out. His anorak caught
fire. I grabbed him back. Tore the anorak off him,
rolled him in a rug. Fortunately he was hardly
hurt at all, hair singed a bit, mainly shocked and
frightened.'

Shelly felt the air go out of her lungs. She could
imagine the moment of excruciating pain, the
panic at the scene. A long golden smudge of late-
afternoon sun dappled the trees in the avenue but
she did not see it. Instead she saw Aidan with his
hand burnt raw, the skin peeling off, trying to
sort out the chaos at the scene of the accident.

'You were very brave,' she said, the words
sticking in her throat. 'It must have been awful.'

'It was purely instinct,' said Aidan. 'Anyone
would have done the same.'

Aidan was holding her hand as if his life
depended on it. There was no question of anyone
letting go. The magic of his touch was unbeliev-
able, his fingers curling round hers. Shelly knew
that the moment had come and she would never
get away from him now. It was here in this idyllic
setting on this beautiful island that she would
destroy the last remnants of affection that Aidan
might feel for her.

'So. . .' he went on, drawing long on the word. 'Just who was it that stole you away from me? It must have been another man. Mel Gibson? I can't think of any other reason.'

'It wasn't another man.'

Her coffee grew cold as she hesitated.

'Shelly, please. . .' His voice was low and distraught. 'Don't torture me like this. Didn't last night mean anything to you? Don't you realise that I still love you? That there's still some future for us? But first there's got to be the complete truth.'

Shelly tried to find the words, denying the cramp that was gripping her stomach. 'Last night was special. It was as if the three years apart just disappeared. But there's no future for us, Aidan, I know that. When you hear what I have to say you'll probably never speak to me again.'

She wanted to cry. She wanted to put her head on the blue tablecloth and howl. Her emotions had been through a shredder in the last few days.

'I always admired you for your high ideals,' she began at last. 'You were full of ideas for saving the world, for curbing disease, for controlling the population in India, Africa. . .all the areas of the world where both disease and population are escalating and threatening the stability of the next generation.'

'I can't work miracles on my own,' said Aidan grimly. 'China is trying with their one child, one family policy. But it's going to come unstuck in a few years when there are no girls for wives and only a small workforce. Go on with the lecture.'

'I knew how strongly you felt about over-population, even in Britain with all the bad housing and lack of jobs.' She looked away from him, unable to meet his eyes. 'It must have been an accident. Probably my fault. We were always so careful. At first I couldn't believe it. . . You were away. . .on some course in the States. I don't remember exactly where. But I knew what your reaction would be when I missed. You would want me to have an abortion.'

Her pulse was hammering as the air tensed between them.

'Are you telling me that you were preg-nant?' His voice was ice-cold, cutting like a knife.

'Yes,' said Shelly.

'And you went away to have an abortion with-out telling me?' He bit on the words tersely, his eyes full of cold fury. 'Didn't I have some rights as the father, if I was the father?'

'Don't be silly. Of course it was your baby. But I thought you would want me to have an abortion. Don't you understand? I went away instead to have the baby. I wanted our child.'

Shelly set her features precisely to match his lack of expression. His face was a mask. No tears now. This was a fight.

'Why didn't you discuss this with me?'

'You were away in the States. Don't you remember? I didn't even know when you would return. You didn't bother to tell me. I had to do something on my own, make arrangements.'

'But obviously you changed your mind,' said Aidan, slamming some money on the table and standing up so abruptly that his chair nearly fell over. 'Or else you wouldn't have been able to cruise around the world for the last three years. Did you give it away, have the child adopted?'

'Have our baby adopted? How dare you? Don't you know me at all?' she said tightly.

'Sometimes I don't believe you are the same woman I loved.' He looked away in disgust.

'I took this job because I needed to forget. Because I wanted to get away and try to dull the pain of losing the baby I cared for so much.' She stared towards Aidan, not really seeing him through the fog of memory, only seeing the perfectly formed doll-like baby she had lost. 'I lost the baby, Aidan. A miscarriage at five months. I lost him.'

'Our baby? You miscarried?' Aidan was stunned. His anger fled and despair filled his heart. 'How could that happen? You were always so fit. A little tired, perhaps. . . Why didn't you come back to Kingham General?'

'It was too late. I couldn't face you,' she said huskily. She was not sure he even heard. Aidan had already gone in his usual silent way. He was striding back to the ship, every bone in his spine rigid with pain.

CHAPTER EIGHT

SOMEHOW Shelly made her way back to the *Clipper Countess*, climbing aboard the local launch with other passengers going across the harbour to the ship. She hardly knew which way she was going, the tiled patterns on the pavements dazzling her eyes. Her feet automatically took her to the immaculate white liner, her haven, her refuge. For once Shelly did not admire the elegant sweep of her bows or the fluttering flags. The passengers shot curious glances at Shelly in her crisp uniform, wondering what she had been doing ashore.

'Everything all right, Doctor?' one asked.

'Fine,' said Shelly with a smile. 'Have you had a nice day?'

'Wonderful. Such a lovely island. Still, I shall be glad to get back on board and put my feet up with a cup of tea.'

'Me too,' Shelly agreed.

Shelly wished a cup of tea would solve her heartache. She had never felt so tense. There was no doubt that she and Aidan would both avoid each other for the last days of the cruise but, in such a confined space, they were bound to cross paths.

Despite the fog of her despair, she remembered

to buy a tablecloth for her mother from one of
the stalls along the quayside. She went through
the motions of choosing something pretty and
embroidered in the local style. Climbing the gangway were more passengers, returning now in
droves, ready for showers and pre-dinner drinks
in one of the bars. But she had evening surgery
ahead of her.

'I don't want to worry you, Doctor,' said
Frances as Shelly went into the medical centre.
'But there are three more crew members down
with temperatures and aches and pains.'

'How many does that make altogether now?'

'Eleven, I think.'

'Eleven! Not exactly an epidemic but more than
a coincidence,' said Shelly, going through the
notes that Frances had put out for her. 'Thank
goodness they're not kitchen staff. All engineers
by the look of it. Perhaps it can be contained.'

'We don't have room for them all here in the
medical centre. We need the other wards for passengers.'

'I'll speak to the chief purser and suggest that
they are confined to quarters. There must be some
way of keeping them separate from the rest of
the crew.' Shelly could see a long evening ahead
of her and she was already tired from the journey
to the airport and then the upsetting scene with
Aidan. 'I could do with a stiff drink.'

Frances laughed. 'That's not like you, Shelly.
How about some tea and a sandwich instead?'

'What a wonderful idea. Order me a tuna and prawn and plenty of salad stuff, please. I don't remember when I last ate properly. It must have been yesterday.'

'You're a fine one to talk about nutrition and sensible diets,' said Frances, checking that there was no one yet in the waiting-room. 'You neglect yourself horribly. It's a wonder you haven't got brittle-bone disease.'

'Osteoporosis is not solely caused by a lack of calcium in the diet,' said Shelly, skimming through the Harrises' notes and bringing them up to date. 'There are other factors. In fact they're trying to research the causes because even children are developing it now. At least they are taking the disease seriously at last. Half the broken bones from falls on ship are caused by brittle bones.'

Shelly raced through surgery that evening. Sunburn was not the number-one complaint from Madeira; it was twisted ankles on the uneven cobblestones and one woman had a suspected fracture of the wrist from a fall. It looked as if she would go home with half of her arm in plaster.

'It wasn't the wine,' the woman insisted. 'Though I'd been to a couple of tastings in the port cellars. It was those rough cobblestones. I just went flying.'

'I'm sure it wasn't the port wine,' said Shelly, making arrangements for Jane to do an X-ray immediately. 'They only give you a thimbleful anyway, not enough to stone a crow.'

As soon as Frances closed the doors on evening surgery, Shelly ate the prawn and tuna sandwiches while filling her medical case with what she might need. The crew quarters were several decks down. A flu epidemic would be alarming. Supposing it spread to the passengers and they returned to Southampton with people too ill to make their own way home? Transportation would be a nightmare to organise. The ship would have to be fumigated before the next cruise. She would not be popular with Captain Bellingham, the management, the shareholders. . .

She took a reviving breath of fresh air on deck before she went below. The *Clipper Countess* had left Madeira far behind and was ploughing the deep seas. And there were other lights at sea. She loved the atmosphere of the ship at night, of people having fun, relishing the excellent food, enjoying a sparkling floor show, and afterwards left to spend the rest of the evening any way they wanted to. Dancing. . .blackjack. . .reading in the library. . .or just watching the stars drift by. . .

'Time off?' Aidan appeared at her side, sliding up without a sound. He was the most soundless person she knew. That secret-service syndrome again. Suddenly he was there, tall and dark and unbelievably handsome, his glasses glinting.

'No,' she said. 'Just taking a breather. I have more work to do tonight. A lot of flu cases among the crew. Not exactly funny.'

'Can we talk some more about this afternoon?' Aidan sounded dangerously withdrawn. She was almost afraid of him. 'I am sorry about the way I reacted. I didn't stop to listen to your side of the story. The thought of our having a baby. . . it just knocked me out. I've always wanted a child. God, Shelly, don't you know how much I would have loved a baby, our baby?'

Shelly was contorted with loss. The silence between them limped into unspoken words. Her distress was so total that the black sea below echoed the feelings in her heart.

'I lost the baby,' she breathed, her eyes closed.

'I know, my darling, my darling girl. That must have been awful for you. Perhaps if I had been there. . .' Aidan's voice was broken, hopeless with a kind of guilt. His arm went round her, not sensually but with human comfort. They swayed for a moment, their arms around each other. 'I might have made a dreadful father. My own father made a real mess of things.'

'I thought you wouldn't want the baby,' Shelly murmured. 'One more child on this overcrowded planet.'

'That was just idealistic talk. I would have wanted our baby,' said Aidan. 'At the right time, when you'd enough hospital experience tucked under your belt. Your career has always been important to me. But you had to achieve what you wanted before starting a family.'

His touch on her skin was so insistent, yet gentle

on her bare arm. A flood of warmth swept over her. Spilled white light touched her eyelids. A night wind caressed their faces. Shelly was unable to sort out her thoughts. She was drowning, not under the sea, but beneath the weight of her guilt.

'I'm trying to understand,' Aidan went on, flinching at the sadness on Shelly's face. 'I realise now why you felt you had to go away. Pregnancy of an unmarried doctor at Kingham General could have been a cause of embarrassment but I'd have sorted that out. Married you. Don't you realise how strong and bossy I can be? I'd have carried you through the awkward moments. In fact, I'd have made damned sure there were no awkward moments. Our baby. . . I'd have done anything, Shelly. Tell me about the baby. . .'

Shelly drew a very deep breath. 'I lost him at five months. It was a boy. He was like a doll, like a tiny celluloid toy from Woolworths. Perfect in every way. . .little arms and legs, all perfectly formed.'

'But why did you miscarry? What was the medical cause?' Aidan was making a big effort not to get emotional. 'Why didn't you contact me when I got back from the States?'

'I was afraid. I knew you would be angry.'

'Then you don't know me. The miscarriage?'

'The placenta got damaged somehow and the baby stopped getting any nourishment. I think it happened when I slipped, getting off a bus a few weeks earlier. It was a bad jolt and I had an uncanny feeling at the time that something might be wrong.' Her eyes were glazed with un-happiness.

'So the womb decided to abort?'

Shelly nodded, remembering the pain and sadness. 'I saw him, of course, but he was too small to hold, just a little person floating in a pool of blood. They took him away. . . I never even knew what happened to him afterwards. It all happened before I could have a say.'

His eyes glittered angrily. 'They just disposed of him? Flushed him down the loo? The system can be so callous. And where were you when all this happened?'

'I was staying with my mother. They took me to a local hospital. They were very kind, really.'

'But I phoned your mother several times,' he said, feeling in his pocket for the absent cigarettes. 'She said she didn't know where you were. I kept phoning her. For months.'

'I know. I told her to say that. I didn't want to see you. It was sheer confusion and I knew you'd be angry with me, the same way that you're angry now. I was the one who was on the Pill. It was my responsibility. I must have forgotten to take it. Sometimes on night duty I hardly knew what I was doing or what time it was.'

'What a mess,' he groaned. 'What a bloody mess.'

Shelly felt the harshness of his breathing rasping over her face. She was unable to speak or move.

The touch of his hand felt like forgiveness but she was not sure. Their need for each other was overflowing. She reached for him hungrily, her lips already parted in anticipation.

But there was a new iron cast to his face. She moved away mindlessly. Never had she known such desolation. She wanted to curl into a ball to protect herself.

'Did you say influenza?' he said with an unrestrained violence. 'Then we'd better get down there.' It was as if something frantic steered his thoughts towards work. It was always a salvation. They were both professionals who knew that work was the only comfort.

'Are you coming with me?'

'Are you going to stop me?'

She shook her head, almost unable to find a voice. And when she did speak it was with a hoarse tenderness that shattered the last of her composure.

'No, never. I could be there all night. Heaven only knows how many of the crew are suffering. Some may not have reported in sick yet.'

It had reached almost epidemic proportions but not quite. They both worked among the crew, tracking the acutely infectious disease, assessing severity of symptoms, doling out paracetamol for the uncomplicated cases. But there were a lot of sick men in their bunks, feeling sorry for themselves. Shelly was desperate that it should not spread to the passengers. Aidan was invaluable with his advice. He knew how important it was to contain the virus, and he had more experience than her in environmental issues.

'We can only put them in standard isolation,' she said hurriedly when they met in a narrow corridor. 'The third engineer has a high fever. He's got to be watched for signs of pneumonia. Fortunately he has his own cabin.'

'Pains in the chest, rapid breath, blueish tinge to the lips. Plenty to drink, light diet.' Aidan reminded himself of basic medicine. He'd been operating for so many years that he'd almost forgotten standard practices. 'Don't worry. We've caught it at the beginning. This is the time to build a wall, make sure it doesn't spread.'

Shelly did not really understand how he was going to do it but she trusted him and was not sorry to leave that part of the organisation to him. It was already halfway through the night and she was desperate for sleep. So was Aidan. Luckily there had been no cabin calls. Their paying passengers were sleeping and dreaming peacefully.

Dawn was tingeing the sky when they finally finished the tricky isolation arrangements. Shelly felt she couldn't take another temperature or check another pulse. She was drained. Her brain was at a standstill.

Aidan bent and kissed her at the door to her cabin. His glasses slipped on his nose and a hinge caught in her hair.

'Whoops,' he said tenderly, releasing her hair

and straightening his glasses with one finger.
'Sleep well. No bad dreams. We can both start
afresh now.'

When he had gone Shelly stood in the doorway,
wondering what he had meant. He had not said
they would start afresh together. And that was
what she wanted to hear.

The reassuring sight of Gibraltar came into view
before breakfast. There was no mistaking the
towering shape of the Rock. Soon the passengers
could have a taste of home with British-style
policemen and telephone boxes and English pubs
while basking in Mediterranean sunshine.

'There's even an M & S,' grinned Jane after
morning surgery. 'I want to stock up on undies.'

'Don't get abducted by one of the Barbary
apes,' said Frances. 'They fancy glossy
shopping bags.'

'At least take the cable car to the top of the
Rock,' said Shelly, finishing her notes. 'There are
some wonderful views from the top.'

'Aren't you coming ashore?' Jane asked.

'Hardly,' said Shelly, stretching her arms. 'Not
with so many of the crew running temperatures.
I shall spend the whole day bathing heated brows.'

'As long as that's all you're bathing,' Frances
teased as she put the instruments in the steriliser.
'Some of those men are rearing to get home. Take
a chaperon with you.'

Shelly stood up, smoothing her skirt. It would
soon be time to change back into her navy uniform

skirt. They were tracking for home now. One more port of call, Bordeaux, and then they would be only a day's cruise away from docking at Southampton. Aidan would return to Kingham General and she would pay a quick visit to see her mother in Bournemouth.

She did not go on deck to see if Aidan was taking Elaine ashore. She took it for granted that he would. It did not bother her any more. He had his own life to lead and if it did not include her then she had brought it upon herself. She was forming permanent pictures of herself in the future. . .alone, a workaholic, spending her life caring for others.

She shook herself mentally. This was stupid. She had work to do and these thoughts were wasting time. The sooner she did her ward rounds, the sooner she could be reclining on a lounger on deck. She had not got beyond chapter one of the novel she had borrowed from the ship's library.

There were no new flu patients, which was a relief. The third engineer was still very unwell but there were no signs of pneumonia. It seemed that the outbreak was contained. Shelly was able to take a light lunch on the pool deck—chicken curry with a side salad, fresh peaches and an ice cream. Afterwards she changed into natural stone linen trousers with a woven striped waistcoat, and took her book up on deck, looking for a discreet hideaway. The fluid lines hid her womanly shape and that was what she wanted.

She stretched out on to a lounger turned towards the sun, unable to believe that she actually had a few hours off. She read a few pages but her eyelids grew heavy and she fell into a light doze. If she dreamed then she did not remember her dream. The sounds from the Rock lulled her into a sense of security, relaxing her tensed muscles. She could smell the scents of Mediterranean flowers—jacaranda, jasmine, honeysuckle. She had once visited Gibraltar's famous public park, the Alameda Gardens, and still remembered the rare flowers on view.

'Doctor, Doctor. It is Dr Smith, isn't it?'

Shelly sat up, instantly wide awake. 'Yes. Hello. Is something the matter? How can I help you?'

A young woman was hovering near the rail, her eyes searching along the deck. She looked distraught. The colour of her face was grey with pain. 'I can't find my son. He was here only a moment ago. I was taking him to the Jig-Saw Club. He's only four and the morning ashore was enough for him.'

Shelly went to the nearest telephone. 'Don't worry, we'll soon find him. What's his name?'

'Jimmy. Jimmy Powell. He's four and has got fair hair.'

Shelly rang straight through to the purser's office. 'This is Dr Smith. I'm reporting a lost child somewhere on the ship. He's four years old, fair-haired and called Jimmy Powell. I think he's too small to have slipped off the ship by himself. Could you put out a call to alert the crew?'

'Of course, Doctor. I'll put out the emergency call.'

Few passengers knew that there was an emergency code system for public announcements. It would not do to have panic spreading through the ship. Every member of the crew hearing the coded phrase would pick up the nearest phone and get recorded information on the lost child. It meant that within seconds all the crew, including bar staff and stewards, were alerted to be on the look-out for Jimmy.

Shelly took Mrs Powell round the decks and public rooms, retracing their steps.

'We returned to the ship for lunch then we went to our cabin to get a clean T-shirt for Jimmy. He'd spilt some juice down it. Messy boy. I went into the bathroom and the next minute he wasn't there. I ran outside. Sometimes he gets so excited about going to the Jig-Saw Club that he can't wait. But he wasn't in sight anywhere. Then I saw you. . .'

'Someone will spot him soon. Where's your husband, Mrs Powell?'

'He's stayed ashore. He wanted to go into the galleries inside the Rock. I didn't fancy them.'

'The ship is a big place but don't worry. We'll find him.' Shelly put confidence into her voice but there were so many nooks and crannies in which a small boy could hide. A steward appeared with a tray of tea for Mrs Powell. Shelly made her sit down and have a cup of tea. It would not help if Mrs Powell became hysterical.

A call came for Shelly from Captain Bellingham. 'I hear you're handling this very well, Doctor,' he said. 'Both gangways are being watched, passenger and crew. Please keep me informed.'

'Thank you, Captain.'

'How is Mrs Powell?'

'As well as can be expected but it'll help when her husband returns. I know that a child on his own could never have slipped by the duty officers at the head of the gangway, but I can't get rid of the feeling that he might have gone looking for his father.'

'I'll contact the police ashore with a description just in case,' said Captain Bellingham.

The *Clipper Countess* was due to set sail for Bordeaux at six p.m. Shelly knew the captain could delay sailing for a short time and make it up during the night, but he could not delay sailing indefinitely.

Shelly left Mrs Powell with Jane and Frances. She kept getting the strangest feeling that they were all looking for Jimmy in the wrong place. Perhaps she had watched too much television. Lost children on board ship were usually spotted within minutes. But this was over an hour now. Surely someone would have seen a small fair-haired boy wandering about?

'We never let children go ashore on their own,' said the duty officer at the head of the gangway. 'They have to be accompanied by a parent. It's a very strict rule.'

'Could a child slip by?' Shelly wondered.

'Never. I always make sure they are with a parent. We have every passenger's cruise card to check off and on. We also make a very accurate numbers check with the counter.'

She saw Aidan returning to the ship, climbing the gangway, tall and relaxed, talking to an elderly couple. Elaine was not with him. He had clearly had a good day.

'Everything all right?' he asked pleasantly, coming over to her. Shelly leaned against a wall, suddenly feeling that she could not rely on her legs to hold her up. She looked into his overly bright eyes. He could make her feel so rapturously alive in seconds. It was total insanity.

'The influenza is under control,' she said, afraid he would move away. She wanted to delay him. She realised with a raw feeling how much she had missed him all day. 'But now we've a small boy lost on board. It's very worrying.'

But it was as if he wasn't listening. Aidan was smiling down at her and it was all she could do to keep her hands off him. She could not even say his name.

'Elaine didn't come with me today,' he grinned. He was teasing her now. 'She said she wanted to rest. My style of sightseeing is too hectic.'

'I never gave her a thought,' said Shelly abruptly. 'I've been far too busy. You're free to go ashore with whom you wish. It's none of my business.'

'I thought you'd say that,' he said, fingering the edge of her waistcoat. 'This is nice. I like the texture. Come and have a drink. I'll buy you an Orchard Dream Fizz in the Ensign bar, non-alcoholic of course. Too early in the day to have you pie-eyed.'

'Don't be daft,' said Shelly, despite being with the person she most wanted to see. 'We must find this little boy first. There's not much time before we're due to sail.'

Aidan's face changed suddenly. 'What did you say? A child missing? How old is he? How long has he been gone?'

Shelly told him quickly but he was already walking towards the main staircase and hurrying down. 'Where are you going?' she shouted after him.

'Elaine. I'm going down to her cabin. She's stolen children before. That's why I've been keeping an eye on her. She's pretty unstable.'

'But why didn't you tell me all this?' said Shelly, running to keep up with him. 'Surely I should have known? I'm supposed to know if any of our passengers have problems.'

'She's supposed to be cured of this obsession for a child. She's had treatment and is currently on medication. I believe she still has therapy at some clinic.'

'You say she's stolen children before?' Shelly couldn't believe that she had heard him properly.

'Yes, twice. A baby from a hospital, then a toddler from a supermarket. This is her cabin.' Aidan knocked on the door. 'Elaine? Elaine? Are you there?' He rattled the handle but the door was locked.

'I'll get her cabin steward,' said Shelly, already making for the stewards' deck station. 'He'll unlock it for me.'

The cabin was empty but on the floor was a small T-shirt stained with orange juice. On the bed was an opened Cellophane packet.

'She's bought a "Clipper Club" T-shirt from the boutique and changed him into it,' said Shelly. 'Small size.'

'And a baseball cap,' said Aidan, spotting the boutique docket. 'Small size.'

'To make him look different.'

They looked at each other, the same thought occurring to both of them. 'She's taken him off the ship.'

Shelly rang straight through to the captain. 'We think that one of the passengers has taken Jimmy ashore. She has changed his appearance. We've found his old shirt in her cabin.' Shelly described the blue club shirt and baseball cap. She also described Elaine. 'In her forties, slim, brown-haired. Rather mouse-like.'

'Or she could still be on board with the boy?'

'I don't think he would stay with her on board.

If he saw his mother he'd run straight to her, or he'd want to go to the Jig-Saw Club. But if Elaine suggested something like "Let's go look for your father", then he might go with her.'

'Is this the young woman Mr Trent warned me about?' said Captain Bellingham. 'He told me she was unstable, had a history.'

'Possibly,' said Shelly, everything falling into place. But there was no time to go into it now.

Shelly and Aidan hurried to the gangway, hoping the duty officer would remember Elaine leaving with a small boy in a baseball cap. But he didn't. Seven hundred passengers coming and going all day. . . It was impossible.

'So that's why you've been going around with Elaine,' said Shelly, slipping her hand into Aidan's as if they had never parted. 'It wasn't. . . anything else.'

'I was just making sure she was all right,' said Aidan, sliding his fingers between hers. 'Keeping an eye on her. She seemed happy and less tense when she was with me. It felt like a good idea.'

'It was a good idea. And thank you,' said Shelly. 'Now we've got to find her. Perhaps we ought to split up.'

'No,' said Aidan firmly. 'It'll need two of us when we find her. She'll need help and maybe the boy will, too. Besides,' and he looked down at her ruefully, 'I don't want the ship to sail without us. They might sail without me, but they wouldn't dare leave you behind.'

'And I thought it was my company you wanted,' smiled Shelly as they hurried down the gangway. She had no make-up on, her hair plaited into a rope. She looked about seventeen, her shapely body tanned and smooth. Aidan averted his glance. He was filled with a deep and sweet compulsion to kiss her there and then in front of everyone. Instead he put her fingers to his moist mouth and touched them lightly.

'I've always wanted your company,' he said roughly.

'We've less than an hour,' said Shelly, changing the subject quickly, but touched to her heart by his gesture. 'She could have taken him across the border to Spain by now.'

'Spain! I'd never thought of that. She's probably got her passport with her. They could be on the bus to Málaga.'

But Elaine hadn't. They spotted her at an open-air café, sitting in the dappled sun and feeding Jimmy an ice-cream sundae.

'My son loves ice cream,' Elaine said, smiling up at Aidan with undisguised contentment. 'I promised him a special one today.'

CHAPTER NINE

SHELLY loved the long days at sea, voyaging across the ocean, the endless, timeless waves washing round the ship. She was at peace with the sea. Maybe that was why she had found refuge working on the *Clipper Countess* after losing her baby.

It had taken her months to accept the grief. Miscarriage was like a bereavement. It was not universally recognised by the medical profession or families that the mother's distress was as real as if she had carried the baby full term. Too often the mother was just prescribed a tranquilliser and left to get on with it.

She always made time for a walk round the decks, relishing the time alone, however active she might be below decks. This morning she felt refreshed after a good night's sleep. Elaine was safely sedated in her cabin with a female member of the crew for company. It could not be Jane or Frances, as they were both far too busy at the medical centre. But others had volunteered the odd hour and a rota had been drawn up by the purser's office.

Jimmy was back with his parents, quite oblivious to the drama that had erupted around him. As far as he was concerned, this nice lady had asked him if he would like an ice cream. He was used to people putting clean clothes on him, so he had thought nothing of the change of shirt. He liked the baseball cap. He wanted to keep it.

'I don't know how we can thank you,' Mrs Powell had said tremulously, hugging her son close to her. 'If it hadn't been for you. . .I can't bear to think what might have happened.'

'You don't have to thank me,' Shelly had said. 'I'm so glad we found Jimmy and that no harm has come to him.'

'That woman must be mad!'

'No. . .not really. She's just very unhappy and disturbed. Of course, that doesn't excuse what she did.'

Shelly was relieved that Aidan's interest in Elaine had been purely professional. But she had to admit to herself that she had been insanely jealous. The sight of Aidan talking to Elaine had been hurtful, like a knife twisting in her stomach. Yet she did not have the slightest hold on Aidan. He was free to talk to whom he pleased.

And he had been talking about Elaine in that overheard conversation with Captain Bellingham. It was obvious now. But it had caused Shelly hours of anguish thinking he was telling the captain about her inexplicable disappearance.

Aidan waved to her briefly from the pool, dark hair sleek and dripping, and that was enough. Strangely, that simple moment of recognition warmed her heart and she caught at his strength and drew the embers close. He gave her the endurance she needed for the day. Perhaps she would see him in the evening. That would be wonderful, a few minutes of his company. . .that was all she asked.

But Aidan sought her out at lunchtime, took her tray from her as she was descending the steps from the pool buffet. He smiled at her, a warm, genuine smile.

'May I help you, madam?' he said, using the steward's jargon. He even copied the Asian accent.

'I keep telling the safety committee that there should be more stewards on pool duty at lunchtime. We've already had one accident,' she said, trying to hide her pleasure at seeing him. He was so brown now, his skin smooth and glistening. His hand was healing beautifully and more mobile with physiotherapy, his eyes rested and sparkling. There was no doubt that the cruise had been beneficial.

'Stop being so professional, Shelly. You're off duty for at least twenty minutes. Stay and have your lunch with me. I've put my things on a table. Can I buy you a Pimm's?' His charm was irresistible.

'Why not?'

He made her sit at the table he had reserved. His lunch tray was there, holding much the same as hers: chicken curry with rice, side salad, fruit and yogurt. Though there was a full five-course meal being served in the dining-room, he seemed to prefer a lighter meal.

Grace Goldsmith waved from across the deck, soup spoon in hand. Shelly waved back. Grace looked happier, so obviously the liquid diet was working for her.

'Don't worry, I've spoken to Miss Goldsmith,' said Aidan, returning from the bar with the long, cold drink. 'I've told her about the association. And I suggested that she should get in touch with me if her GP has trouble with her treatment. There is absolutely no need for her to suffer from her condition.'

'You're wonderful,' said Shelly, the first sip of her Pimm's going straight to her head. They made a potent Pimm's in the ship's bars.

'Now that's exactly the kind of thing I need to hear,' Aidan chuckled, looking at her with such longing that Shelly wondered if she could hold on to her reason. Her spine began to tingle and it was not just the early-day alcohol. He was devouring her with his eyes. She dug the fork into her salad, hoping she would be able to collect her wits before she made a fool of herself.

How could she have got into this state again? She loved him. She adored him. Aidan, Aidan. . . She would lay down her life for him. And he had invited her to lunch, bought her a Pimm's. Did that mean anything? No, he was just being his usual charming and polite self.

But were his eyes saying more than that? Shelly

knew that she wanted to share his life. But he hadn't said that, had he? He had said he was sorry about the baby, sympathised and been genuinely upset. But that was over now. All part of the past. And that was how it had to be. She understood but wished it could have been different.

They talked about all sorts of things. Half an hour of friendly talk. It was therapeutic. Shelly would go back to her work with her heart singing. Aidan had been devastatingly sweet, unbearably tender. It was almost more than she could cope with.

'I have to go. The crew flu calls.'

'How are they?'

'Recovering, although the third engineer is still poorly. He's been really ill. But he's feeling better today.'

'And how about Elaine?'

'I've made sure she has round-the-clock company. And she can go on deck if she has two people with her. I think she'd been forgetting to take her medication. She seemed to have quite a stock of pills. I saw her first thing this morning and she was very quiet and docile. She didn't seem to remember much about Jimmy at all, as if it had been a dream.'

'Sad case,' said Aidan. 'She needs a lot of help, a lot of support.'

'Which unfortunately the NHS can't give her.'

'The Ensign bar at six p.m.?' he said, leaving her at the head of the stairs. 'Shall we meet there?'

'If surgery is over.'

'I'll wait for you.'

He turned and went back up on deck. She saw his hand go to his shirt pocket and take out a packet of cigarettes. He shook one out then put it back. She was dismayed. Had Aidan started smoking again? Was it her fault? Perhaps what she had told him affected him so deeply that he had fallen prey to nicotine addiction again. She felt chilled and sick that she might be the cause.

Shelly made herself settle to writing her report for Head Office. She had let her paperwork get behind; this was a good opportunity to catch up.

Halfway through the afternoon she was called to a bad fall at the ballroom-dancing class. She was not surprised. There was quite a swell and keeping balance during tricky dance steps was difficult when the polished floor was tipping in all directions.

She hurried to the lounge where the classes were held. A crowd had gathered round the injured dancer, a good-looking woman in her late forties, a little overweight and wearing a full-skirted sundress. Her face was screwed up with pain. The two dancing teachers were hovering over her anxiously. Injuries were their nightmare.

'I hope I haven't broken anything,' the woman groaned. 'I have to go back to work on Monday.'

Shelly examined her leg carefully. It was twisted under her in an awkward position.

'And to think I saved up for a whole year for

this cruise,' the woman went on, licking the sweat off her upper lip. 'I should have gone to Minehead. It would have been safer.'

'Don't worry,' said Shelly, carefully straightening the leg. The thigh area was very tense. 'I don't think you've broken anything. It looks more like a pulled tendon. Very painful, I'm afraid, but we'll get you down to X-Ray just to make sure.'

'Thank you, Doctor. What a silly thing to happen. We were learning the Boston Two-Step.'

'You couldn't help it. We've got a quartering sea. The ship's movement is a bit unpredictable.'

The woman was looking more cheerful now that she knew she hadn't broken anything. Her dancing partner was being most solicitous and she obviously liked his attention. Perhaps their shipboard friendship was about to move into a different gear.

'I'll come with you, Linda,' he said. 'I'll bring your handbag.'

It was Cyril Howard, the widower with arthritis. Shelly had heard that he was about to win the super quiz again, but she didn't know he had added dancing to his achievements.

Another crowd, bigger and more excited, had gathered by the port-side rails. They were all talking and pointing. The video enthusiasts were out filming.

'What's happened?' Shelly asked a passing steward.

'Tuna,' he said and shrugged.

'You mean a shoal of dolphins?'

'No, fishermen. A fishing boat, I think.'

'What do you mean?'

It was hopeless trying to get any information out of him. Shelly would find out for herself after she had made Linda more comfortable. She remembered reading in the ship's daily newspaper something about a tuna war but had not had time to read the item properly.

Her surgery phone rang. It was the deputy captain.

'Can you come, Doctor? We've got an emergency—some injured fishermen in a boat. We're lowering number eight launch to take you out to it.'

'Right,' said Shelly. She could leave Linda in Jane's capable hands. 'Port side? I'll be there right away.'

The phone rang again as soon as she had put down the receiver. It was Aidan. She knew instinctively it would be him.

'Have you heard?'

'Yes. The tuna war. I'm on my way.'

'Get your staff to bring duplicates of everything,' he said crisply. 'All the emergency equipment.'

'I've back-up of everything.'

'Bring it all along. There's going to be enough work for both of us. I'll see you at the launch side. . .number eight launch. I mean, if you want me to be there?' For once he did not sound so

sure of himself. The great Aidan Trent had something else on his mind.

'I do, but tell me what's happened?' she asked
urgently, but he had already rung off. She
whipped off her skirt and stepped into a pair of
cotton navy trousers she kept in a locker in the
surgery. They would be easier to work in on a
trawler. Injured fishermen. . .she did not like the
sound of that.

It was so like Aidan to assume that she would
want him along. But he was right. She couldn't
manage on her own and there was no point in
taking Jane or Frances.

'What's happened?' said Frances, catching
her arm.

'I haven't the slightest idea. No one has told
me. Just get everything movable to number eight
launch. And the sea-rescue stretchers. We'll
need them.'

'I'm coming with you.'

'You can't. There's no way I can leave the
Clipper Countess without adequate medical staff-
ing. We might have more casualties from the
Boston Two-Step. It looked pretty lethal.'

'We'll be on the deck ready to move anyone
down to the medical centre.'

'That would be really useful. Get the wards
ready,' Shelly said, before contacting the deputy
captain for any more information on the injuries.

The trawler was riding the swell not far from
the *Clipper Countess*. She was flying distress flags.

Her name, *Lobelia*, was clearly readable on her bows. A crowd of fishermen were leaning over the rails and waving vigorously at the cruise ship.

More passengers gathered at the rails to watch the drama. They evidently thought this was better than the film showing in the cinema that afternoon.

'Oh, dear, we've got an audience,' said Shelly, climbing into the launch. Aidan was already sitting on one of the benches wearing a life-jacket; he knew that boarding the trawler might be tricky. He helped Shelly get into hers, crossing the straps of the bulky jacket and tying them firmly.

'Can't have you falling in the brink,' he said. 'Do we know what's happened yet?'

'I thought you knew everything. An axe wound and a heart attack, I think. The message was garbled. Thank you for coming with me, Aidan. I appreciate your help,' she said, trying to ignore the powerful feelings swirling inside her.

'An axe wound? Good heavens, what's that all about?' he asked anxiously. 'Has someone gone berserk?'

'I hope it isn't a head wound,' said Shelly, gazing ahead to the trawler. 'Don't you read your daily ship's newspaper? There was an item about a tuna war going on between the French and Spanish fishermen and the British trawlers in the Bay of Biscay.'

'I came on this cruise to get away from the

world's troubles. I vowed I wouldn't even open a newspaper, not even a mini-paper,' he said, his eyes raking over her gently. Shelly wished she could eliminate the inches that separated them but the bulky jackets and curious crew made her move even further away.

'You've started smoking again,' she accused, regretting the words immediately.

'No, I haven't. I only bought a packet,' he said casually, frowning, dismissing her reproach. 'Why should you care? You made your decision about our relationship three years ago when you walked out without trusting me. We have to get on with living. Anything wrong with that?'

'No, of course not. You know what you're doing.' She was lost for words. She was treading on dangerous ground. She made an effort to control the storm of emotion that threatened to engulf her. She may as well put him right out of her life as she had once before. 'Sorry I spoke. But please don't smoke around my patients.'

He sent her a withering glance, his eyes snapping like slate behind the glasses, not bothering to reply. His look chilled her. She hated it when he looked at her with such scorn.

The trawler was getting closer. Shelly could see that the mahogany wheelhouse had been destroyed, the door smashed, and other parts of the deck seemed to have been hacked at. Everywhere was wrecked.

Shelly was not looking forward to boarding the

trawler. No one had trained her for nautical acrobatics.

But the crew of the launch were trained and by some miracle they manoeuvred near enough for Shelly to leap across with a leading line into the ready arms of some sturdy Cornish fisherman. She did not watch Aidan taking the same perilous route but went immediately to the first injured fisherman, who was lying under an awning on the slippery deck. The smell of fish was powerful and she tried to blank her mind to it. The man was bleeding furiously from a gaping wound in his leg. The crew had tried to staunch it with towels but they were soon soaked in blood.

'Axes and crowbars and sledgehammers,' said the unshaven skipper, his face ashen, wiping off the sweat. 'They just came aboard the *Lobelia* and started smashing everything up. Charlie here got in the way. Axe sliced his leg badly. And old Joe. . .you gotta do something about him, Nurse.'

Shelly didn't bother to correct him; it wasn't important. Charlie's life was important. The blood was welling up in a steady stream, soaking his jeans. It spurted from the wound in time with his heartbeats. Aidan went straight to the older man, who was lying unconscious on the deck.

Shelly lifted the injured leg and propped it on a pile of nets. She pressed hard on the wound, using a firm pad dressing. She applied a standard dressing but blood was still seeping through. It needed a second, bigger dressing on top of that, bandaged even more firmly.

'Ain't you gonna stitch it up?'

'Yes, when I get Charlie back on board ship. It's important first to stop the bleeding and clean the wound.' Shelly set up a saline drip into the man's arm. 'Hold this, will you?' She called over a frightened-looking youth. He needed something to do to take his mind off the attack.

The lad was shaking but he took the line and began talking nervously. 'It was awful. There was about forty Spanish boats all round us. They came alongside, shouting and everything and hacked away at our nets. Then they sank them with anchors and weights.'

'We didn't stand a chance,' the skipper chimed in. 'They were shouting at us and waving axes about. Then they came aboard. It was terrifying. Like being attacked by pirates.'

'It must have been awful. Where are you from?' Shelly asked, checking Charlie's blood pressure and pulse. He needed a transfusion quickly. He was lucky that the axe had not severed an artery.

'Penzance. I been fishing here for thirty years. They're trying to force us out of these seas.'

'Fishing's our livelihood. They can't force us out. We gotta right to fish.'

She stumbled over piles of slashed nets, sliding on fish scales, calling out to the launch. The sea was rough and the trawler was pitching quite a lot. Seagulls swooped and screeched. 'Get a couple of the Neil Robertson stretchers over here. Can you cope with the transfer of the patients if we strap them in?'

'OK, Doctor. Leave it to us,' the officer shouted back. 'Stretchers coming over.'

Aidan had turned Joe over into the recovery position and cleared debris from the airway with a sucker so he could breathe. The fisherman's breathing was heavy and laboured, and one side of his face had sagged. Aidan quickly made a general examination.

'It's a stroke, not a heart attack,' said Aidan. 'He's an old man. There's not a lot we can do here. I want to put in a Geudal airway. Size four. Have you got one?'

Shelly handed him the airway and watched Aidan slip it smoothly and gently into Joe's mouth.

'I'll go back with Joe. He mustn't be left alone,' said Aidan. 'He could lapse into a coma.'

'The crew are in shock and there a lot of minor injuries, cuts and bruises. They all need to come back to the ship for hot baths and tea and patching up. They'll want to get messages home to their families. We'll get the deputy captain to put a holding party on board the trawler till the skipper feels able to take the *Lobelia* back to Penzance. She's damaged but still seaworthy.'

'And all because their fishing nets are too long,' said Aidan harshly. 'Those EC rules.'

'But the British nets are longer because they

include gaps to allow dolphins to escape,' Shelly pointed out.

The stout Neil Robertson stretchers were ideal for the transfer. There was plenty of help to lift the men on to the canvas and wooden slates and strap them in safely.

They were too busy with their patients to talk much on the precarious launch trip back to the *Clipper Countess*. Shelly wanted the two men in the medical centre, where she could treat them properly. So far it had been simple first aid for both men.

The video cameras were running. The passengers were taking advantage of real drama to spice up their home movies. Aidan seemed annoyed by the attention from above. His face was stony but he said nothing.

Although Aidan was being perfectly polite and considerate, Shelly could feel that he was distancing himself from her. They would be docking at Southampton the day after Bordeaux and she guessed he wanted it to be a complete break. Her heart seemed to stop for a split-second. She could not imagine a future for herself without Aidan. But the hard set of his face told her that this was not the time to say anything.

Perhaps she would never say anything. Perhaps it was already too late. Those magic moments together that night might have been Aidan's way of saying goodbye.

She turned her face to the wind so that Aidan

would not see the tears in her eyes. Loving some-one who did not love you was painful.

The two injured men were lifted aboard the cruise ship and then the launch went back for other members of the crew. Once in her medical centre, Shelly and Aidan were able to do so much more. Charlie's bleeding was staunched and it was time to undertake definitive treatment. There was damage to the underlying tissue and muscle. Shelly sutured the wound using silk thread, bring-ing together the deeper tissue, cutting the ligature ends short. She gave standard antibiotic treatment and a tetanus injection; there was no way of know-ing what else that axe had been used for.

She left Frances to put on the sterile gauze dressing and bandaging. 'Elevate the leg to encourage draining and reduce swelling,' she said. 'And bring Charlie a cup of tea, please. He deserves it.'

Charlie was smiling stiffly. 'My wife'll never believe this,' he said. 'Me on a posh cruise ship. Hospital and all.'

'You're going to be all right. You've lost a lot of blood but the body has a wonderful way of making it up.'

'You're not going to give me a trans-fusion, then?'

'We've been successful in stemming the blood. The bleeding is controlled now. Your pulse and blood pressure are improving. Plenty of liquid is the answer.' She did not tell him that they did not have his blood type on board. She would have to go through the crew records to find a donor.

'I could do with a pint of cider.'

'I think we could even manage that,' Shelly promised with a smile. 'Our bars are wonderful.'

She still had other patients to look after and evening surgery was imminent. Time had flown. The Ensign bar at six p.m.? Aidan had to be joking. Neither of them would make it and she did not really know if she wanted to keep the date. The image of Aidan always made her yearn for him. She kept seeing his tall figure everywhere on ship, slightly stooping and so darkly handsome, her memory playing uncomfortable tricks.

She wondered if Aidan would remember his invitation or if his change of mood during the afternoon had blotted it out of his mind. Suddenly she was too tired to care. If he didn't want her in his life then this was the end of their romance. She would make a new life for herself. She would make sure that their paths never crossed again.

CHAPTER TEN

THE slow early-morning cruise up the River Garonne was fascinating. One river bank was a stretch of idyllic French countryside, green and serene, while the other bank was a jumble of industrial buildings. Ahead on a wide curve of the great river was the elegant port of Bordeaux with its fine four-storey Louis XV-style houses and showpiece city squares and statues.

Shelly was not going to be seeing any of it. She had forgotten she was down for the inflated-dingy exercise this trip. No one really enjoyed this exercise. The best part was a swim in the hotel pool afterwards but Shelly would far rather have strolled round the harmonious squares of the city, admiring the eighteenth-century buildings and the fortified medieval gateways.

'Let's get it over with quickly,' she said, climbing aboard the minibus that was transporting them to a hotel on the outskirts of Bordeaux. She did not look at the row of coaches that were taking the passengers on wine tours of the Bordeaux region or to place de la Comédie in the city centre and dropping them outside the Grand Théâtre. She knew Aidan would have planned to wander round the city. Instead she watched, with a degree

171

of dread, the deflated and folded rubber dingy being loaded on to a trailer.

'Doctor, I think I'm getting a splitting headache,' said one of the young bar stewards. Every member of the crew including catering staff had to be trained in the procedure of righting an overturned dingy.

'Aren't we all?' said Shelly. 'I've plenty of aspirin. Don't worry, no one likes doing this.'

At least the dreaded exercise underwater kept her mind off Aidan. But already she was feeling an acute loneliness and the jokes and banter of the other crew members went over her head.

She did not spend any of the last evening with Aidan. She caught sight of him propping up the Ensign bar talking into the small hours, drinking Coke most of the time. Seeing him, unseen, gave her a twisted pleasure. Shelly leaned over the rail at the stern of the ship, watching the foamy wake, shivering slightly. The shipping lanes were busy and there were distant lights on the horizon. Bright stars chased each other in the water, darting like silver minnows.

Shelly said goodbye to her patients before they disembarked. Some had already forgotten her help and hurried down the gangways early to catch trains or planes or pick up their cars from the long-stay car park.

She spent extra time with the wheelchair father who had not once asked for medical help even though he was so ill. The family had coped with every contingency themselves and she was glad to learn that they had all enjoyed themselves. But there was still that element of anger in the father's eyes and she didn't blame him. Life was being unfair.

Mrs Scott-Card had had to buy an extra suitcase.

'I've had a lovely time,' she told Shelly. 'And we are both going on a diet as soon as we get home. Your diet sheet doesn't look too bad.'

'Good,' said Shelly. 'Slow and steady, that's the way. No crash diets or fad foods.'

Nicky, the asthmatic girl, was saying a tearful goodbye to a handsome young officer from the purser's office. Shelly knew that in a month or so the cruise would just be a lovely dream and Nicky would recover. Shelly had lost count of the officer's number of tearful goodbyes over the year. The ship was a floating school for junior officers and cadets and the young girls were never short of dancing partners.

As soon as the last passengers were off she would change out of uniform and phone her mother to say she was coming home. She was not due back on board until five p.m. the following day. That gave her a clear thirty hours. The fast turn-around was a mammoth operation, with staff working at speed to be ready for the intake of seven hundred new passengers.

Aidan had already gone ashore without speak-

ing to her. She spotted him on the dockside,
seeing Elaine into a car, watched him with an
aching emptiness. He looked every inch the
London consultant now in a well-cut city suit and
black T-shirt. . .his halfway gear, as he called
it, his trademark at Kingham General. Elaine
was clinging to him but Aidan was trying to
disentangle himself without being impolite.

Shelly sighed. Well, it was truly all over now.
Their magical Indian summer. Perhaps she had
begun to nurture silly hopes of their getting
together again but Aidan had made it very clear
since Gibraltar that he had finished with her. He
had been distancing himself in an obvious way.

She said goodbye to Jane, who was staying on
board to take the dispensary delivery for the next
cruise and check everything.

'Have a nice time ashore,' said Jane. 'I'll see
to the delivery and make sure they sent what you
ordered.'

'I feel like doing something normal,' said
Shelly, locking up her files.

'Like the washing-up after supper?' Jane
grinned. 'We get spoilt being waited on all
the time.'

'I still remember how to do it,' said Shelly. 'You
use water and detergent, don't you?'

'Have you said goodbye to your handsome surgeon from Kingham General?' Jane asked. 'Oh,
you don't need to deny it,' she went on with a
warning look. 'When he came to have his hand

dressed he talked of no one but you. What a great doctor you were at Kingham General but that he would never understand you. He asked me if you had a boyfriend hidden away somewhere in your life. He sounded very much like a man who had you on his mind.'

'That's ridiculous,' said Shelly flatly. 'We were just friends. . .of a sort.'

'That wasn't my impression,' said Jane. 'He was full of pent-up emotion and it wasn't all anger. I think he's in love with you.'

'Your imagination's gone into overdrive,' said Shelly lightly. 'I've obviously been giving you too much time off. Nose to the grindstone next cruise.'

Aidan still in love with her, never! Not after the way she had treated him. Shelly did not delude herself. His fury had been real enough even if he had had three years in which to cool down. His love had cooled too, she had no doubt. Nor did she blame Aidan. She had treated him badly but with good reason.

She changed into her linen trousers, teamed this time with a long V-necked silky sweater in cable-knit. They were back in the unpredictable English weather. She tied her hair back with a scrunchie and picked up her overnight bag, checking that she had packed the tablecloth from Madeira. The face in the mirror looked wan, the eyes huge and haunted. Her mother would think she had had too many late nights.

Dino was grinning enormously. 'Surprise for you, Doctor,' he said. Her steward brought a large arrangement of carnations and roses in a fancy basket into her cabin. Aidan! Immediately she felt her heart lurch as if it had turned over, though she knew that was a physical impossibility.

The flowers were from Mr and Mrs Harris with many thanks for her care. Shelly was glad because the gift of flowers meant that they had both reached home safely and were on the mend.

'Heavens,' she said, sniffing their fragrance. 'My cabin will smell like a florist's shop.'

She went down the crew gangway, swinging her bag. English ground felt good. Safe and ordinary. She looked back at the great sweep of the bows of the white lady, loving the clean line of her, but knowing that she was just a floating dream.

'Taxi, lady?'

She swung round, bumping her bag. It was Aidan, standing by a gleaming grey XJ12 Jaguar. his eyes were dark and glinting but they held a wary warmth and invitation in their depths. She hesitated, wondering if she should make a run for it. She was not sure if getting into his car would be a good idea.

'Going anywhere near the station?' she asked tremulously, still not decided. 'I'm catching a train.'

'I'm going to Bournemouth if that's any help?'

She sighed. She could not resist him. Surely she

could handle a few miles in a car and, anyway, he would be driving.

'How come you're going to Bournemouth when that's where I'm going? You've no reason to go to Bournemouth.'

Aidan took her bag and slung it on to the back seat. 'Funny, anywhere you're going, I'm going too,' he said with scant regard for grammar. 'Is that all right?'

Shelly nodded, not trusting herself to speak. She settled herself into the front passenger seat, thrown by his closeness, and fastened the safety belt. She looked at his strong hands, all healed now, resting on the steering wheel. He would be back to work soon, if not on Monday. He started the engine and drove carefully out of the dock area.

'This is a new car,' she said at last. 'Very nice. Better than your ancient old Rover.'

'I've stopped saving money,' he said aggressively. 'Nothing to save for any more. No incentive. My incentive walked out on me. Remember?'

'You can stop at the next corner and let me get out if you are going to launch into a lecture,' said Shelly. 'I thought we had a civilised truce.'

'The truce is over,' said Aidan curtly. 'It was only for the cruise. We're on British soil now and the terms are different.'

Shelly was chilled by the tone of his voice. How could she have thought that he had forgiven and forgotten? No way; the anger and rage were still there, where they had been bottled up for a long time, waiting to erupt.

'Are you going to see your mother?' he went on. 'Have you got the tablecloth or whatever it was?'

'How do you know I bought a tablecloth?'

'I saw you buying it and guessed it was for her. I was making sure you got back. Do you think she'll forgive the way I treated her daughter a few days ago? When I stormed off and let you return to the ship on your own? That was absurdly insensitive of me, especially after you telling me about the baby. I was thrown, I'll admit. I couldn't think straight.'

'I think she will,' said Shelly, not daring to look at him. The air was fragile with promise. 'I have.'

'But I haven't forgiven you,' he said suddenly, shattering that fragile promise. 'I haven't forgiven you for not loving me enough to trust me. You should have told me,' he said roughly. 'Why didn't you trust me? It was so cruel, just going off, sending me that damned stupid note. Didn't you give me a single thought? What do you think I went through, not knowing where you were? Accidents, abduction, hostage situations. . .I went through the lot. I almost expected a ransom note through the post. I drove the local police station mad with my enquiries till your note came. A note that said nothing. It was cruel.'

'You told the police?' Shelly swallowed hard.

'Of course,' he snapped. 'I reported you as a missing person. What did you think I would do? Cross out your phone number and start dating a new nurse? Shelly, I don't think you've any idea what you put me through.'

'What about me?' said Shelly, choking back the tears. 'What do you think I went through? I lost both you and the baby. I was devastated. I wanted that baby. He was all I had of you. Aidan, if we are going to fight all the way to Bournemouth then I'd really rather go by train.'

'You planned it all very carefully, didn't you? Gave your notice in to the hospital management, gave up the lease of your flat, packed your things. The police said you were not a missing person, since everything pointed to a calculated departure.'

'I didn't want you to know about the baby,' said Shelly wretchedly. 'I thought you would insist on an abortion. I hardly knew what I was doing. I just wanted to protect the baby from you.'

'But I was the baby's father!' he raged. 'I had a right to know.'

Shelly trembled with distress. 'How was I to know?' she whispered. 'For years you'd been saying there should be fewer children in the world and I believed you. How could I tell that we were the exception?'

'You should have talked to me!' he exploded. 'I might have been the world's worst father but I

would have tried. Our son would have been so
important to me.'

'Is that why you always said you never wanted
children?' Shelly asked cautiously.

'I had a rotten father. He had no time for us
kids. I was afraid it might run in the family.' He
shook his head in defeat.

'But you kept going on about the world
population. . .'

'It's a global problem that won't go away. But
our baby would have been different, Shelly. If
only you had waited till I'd got back from the
States.'

'It was too much of a risk. I didn't want to be
there when you got back. I had to go. I was afraid
you'd talk me into an abortion and I wanted our
baby desperately. Everything was fine till I fell in
the street. My mother was so helpful, looking
after me.' Shelly's voice was ragged with emotion.

'Your mother said you weren't there!' he
exploded.

'You never came down to check!'

'I believed her. Why should I expect that nice
lady to be lying to me? My word, I was completely
taken in. But why give up your job and your flat?'

'Will you never understand? I loved you so
much, it would have been difficult to resist you.
Don't you know how persuasive you are? I had
to put distance between us so that you would
never know and I could go ahead and bring up
our child.'

'You didn't give me a chance,' said Aidan, gripping the steering wheel hard. 'We'd have worked something out.'

'You tell me that now, when it's too late. Aidan, slow down. You're driving too fast. Please, Aidan. . .'

Shelly saw the junction ahead, seconds before Aidan did.

The car slithered across the road as Aidan swerved to avoid another car crossing at a minor junction. He slammed on the brakes. Shelly clutched at her seat belt.

'You're driving much too fast,' she cried out in anguish. 'You shouldn't drive when you're angry. It's dangerous. Let's stop somewhere and have a coffee. Please, Aidan, slow down. You're frightening me.'

He looked round and saw the fear in her shadowed eyes. And he saw the sadness and despair. There was no denying that Shelly had suffered. It was etched all over her face, her cheekbones finely hollowed.

'You're right,' he said more soberly, driving with care. 'I wouldn't want to dent my new car.'

He turned off the A35, somewhere in the New Forest, and drove to a small Hampshire village where an old mill had been converted into a café. Shelly found that her legs were unsteady as she got out of the car. She did not know what she was doing here with Aidan. She should be on a train, halfway to her mother's home by now.

'I've asked them to bring out some coffee into the garden,' said Aidan, steering her through a small side-gate into a garden. 'Let's go and walk by the stream. You can push me in if I overstep the mark.'

He took her hand in the old way and began to walk alongside the meandering stream. 'Not talking and not communicating is the cause of lots of problems,' he went on. 'I suppose we never had time to talk. Believe me, I would never hurt you. There's so much pain locked up inside me that I have to get rid of it somehow.'

'Are you getting rid of it?' she asked hopefully.

'Some of it. Now that I know the truth.'

And what about my hurt? Shelly thought, but she bit back the words.

Aidan pulled her into his arms. 'You little fool,' he groaned. 'I love you, don't you know that? I still love you, whatever you've done to me. We were always meant to be together. Nothing has changed that. All I want to do is cradle you in my arms and tell you how much I love you and look after you for every last remaining moment of my life.'

It was a long speech for Aidan. In the stillness Shelly could hear the murmur of the stream trickling over pebbles and somewhere a bird throwing his song at the sky.

He kissed her gently, tasting her lips, moving his mouth lightly over her skin, fanning her face with his breath, running his hands through her hair. Her heart was beating hysterically. 'I can never have enough of you, darling. Promise you'll never leave me again. I want to look after you and take care of you. Will you let me?'

'I want to believe you,' she said, confused by Aidan's change of attitude and the giddy sweetness of his kiss. 'But is this the same man who hasn't spoken to me for two days? Not a single word. Not even a casual hello or how are you?'

'I know. It was deliberate. I resolved that I had to try and live without you, Shelly. Cut you out of my life. I kept reminding myself that you might run out on me again. But it isn't possible. I want you with me always, on any terms.'

'But you've been giving me the cold shoulder, very successfully. I'm all frozen down one side,' she said, her face against his arm, nuzzling into his warmth, running her hands down the fabric of his jacket, feeling the muscles beneath.

'Don't remind me,' he said tautly, tilting her face. 'I tried to ignore you but it was useless. You're under my skin, Shelly, and I can't live without you. I want you in my life and I don't care what you do or what you say, but just promise you won't leave me again.'

His voice was ringing with sincerity and longing. Shelly felt the planet spinning beneath her feet. 'There's a lady bringing out our coffee,' she said weakly. 'She'll see us.'

'Who cares? I want the world to see us.'

He took her in his arms so hastily that his

glasses were knocked askew. He took them off and put them in his jacket pocket and with that gesture his face lost a decade. He kissed her as if he had never kissed her before. He never wanted to stop, kissing her lips, her face, her throat. Shelly was the anchor of his life.

He was kissing her frantically as if time counted and life was running out. Shelly understood his panic but tried to calm him with her hands. The kissing went on and on till they had to break for breath.

'I'll never leave you again,' she gasped against his cheek. 'I promise, Aidan, darling. Don't worry, please, my love. . .everything will be all right. We're together again and this time it's forever. . .'

He drew back, searching her face. 'Do you mean that?'

'Yes, I do. You're the only man for me. The only man I want and the only man I love. I tried to forget you in work but I've missed you so much.'

'I know this isn't as romantic as a starlit deck, Dr Smith, just a café garden somewhere off the A35, but will you marry me? I want to share my life with you. I want you to be with me always. I want to make love to you and make a home with you and have babies. . .'

The woman coughed discreetly. 'Your coffees, sir. I've put them on the table. They'll be getting cold.'

'Thank you,' said Shelly as the woman left them.

'You haven't answered me,' he said urgently.

'Darling, it's all I've ever wanted,' said Shelly, touching the dear shape of his dark head. 'Marriage, if that's what you want. Yes, yes, every time.'

'It's what our child will need, a stable family environment, even with a mother who's probably set on keeping her own career in orbit, dammit.'

'I can't waste all that knowledge, all that experience,' Shelly faltered. 'You do understand, don't you? But I could take a year off. . .I think even doctors get maternity leave.'

'Doesn't the shipping line use locums? What happens when you take holiday leave? You could work as a locum. Someone has to stand in,' said Aidan. His face had cleared; he was laughing, touching her cheek tenderly. 'But don't let's worry about it now. We can work it out—careers, family, a home. Nothing is impossible. Bournemouth for lunch, darling. We'll take your mother out. I know the perfect place.'

Aidan also knew the perfect hotel for the night. It was everything that Shelly had ever dreamed about. When he reached for her full and rosy breasts in the cool dusk air of their room she turned to him, heavy with love and unbearable longing. This man was the reason for her existence. This man was her destiny. The ceiling became a scattering of stars as the night retreated into dawn. She shared his breath, his skin, his hair, his weight, his folding limbs, holding nothing back, giving him her whole being.

The elegant white *Clipper Countess* was due to sail from Southampton the next evening at six p.m. Aidan had got Shelly back in time, but only just. He'd had to drive fast. They had lingered over a late lunch, never wanting to part, hands clamped together. Now they kissed and stood close on the dockside. It would be two weeks before they saw each other again.

'Thank goodness this is a shorter cruise,' said Aidan huskily. 'I don't think I could stand anything longer.'

'I'll write and I'll phone from the ship. And I'll take some leave soon,' she promised, blinking back the tears. 'I can check the dates. Then we'll be together all the time. Goodbye, darling. Take care. I love you.'

She turned away abruptly, a sailor's farewell. Swift and painful. It was the only way when it hurt so much.

Shelly stood on the deck as the great liner began to ease away from the docks, helped by a stumpy tugboat. The new passengers were crowding the rails, throwing streamers and waving to their friends ashore. Soon the sides of the ship were festooned with fluttering paper and the water below swimming with swirls of coloured weed.

The Regimental Hampshire and Dorset Band,

1st Battalion, was on the quay playing stirring Sousa marches, the sun bouncing off their brass instruments.

Aidan was a tall, straight figure, standing alone, rays of evening sun still glinting on his glasses like needles long after his beloved features had blurred in the distance.

'Take care, my darling,' Shelly said to the warm southwesterly wind. 'I'll be back soon. Then I'll never leave you again.'

She waved and the man on shore saluted once more.

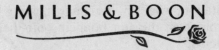

MILLS & BOON

MEDICAL ROMANCE

LOVE ON CALL

The books for enjoyment this month are:

A FRESH DIAGNOSIS	Jessica Matthews
BOUND BY HONOUR	Josie Metcalfe
UNEXPECTED COMPLICATIONS	Joanna Neil
CRUISE DOCTOR	Stella Whitelaw

Treats in store!

Watch next month for the following absorbing stories:

AND DAUGHTER MAKES THREE	Caroline Anderson
A QUESTION OF TRUST	Maggie Kingsley
THE DISTURBING DR SHELDON	Elisabeth Scott
CONSULTANT CARE	Sharon Wirdnam

Available from W.H. Smith, John Menzies, Volume One,
Forbuoys, Martins, Woolworths, Tesco, Asda, Safeway and
other paperback stockists.

Readers in South Africa - write to:
IBS, Private Bag X3010, Randburg 2125.

Happy Mother's Day

Don't miss this year's exciting Mother's Day Gift Pack—4 new
heartwarming romances featuring three babies and a wedding!

The Right Kind of Girl	Betty Neels
The Baby Caper	Emma Goldrick
Part-Time Father	Sharon Kendrick
The Male Animal	Suzanne Carey

This special Gift Pack of four romances is priced at just £5.99

(normal retail price £7.96)

 Available: February 1996   *Price:* £5.99

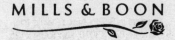

MILLS & BOON

MILLS & BOON

By Request

Bestselling romances brought back to you by popular demand

Two complete novels in one volume
by bestselling author

Roberta Leigh

Two-Timing Man

◆

Bachelor at Heart

Available: March 1996   Price: £4.50

Fl wer
P wer

How would you like to win a year's supply of simply irresistible romances? Well, you can and they're free! Simply unscramble the words below and send the completed puzzle to us by 31st August 1996. The first 5 correct entries picked after the closing date will win a years supply of Temptation novels (four books every month—worth over £100).

1	LTIUP	TULIP
2	FIDLADFO	
3	ERSO	
4	AHTNYHCI	
5	GIBANOE	
6	NEAPUTI	
7	YDSIA	
8	SIIR	
9	NNAIATCRO	
10	LDIAAH	
11	RRSEOIMP	
12	LEGXFOOV	
13	OYPPP	
14	LZEAAA	
15	COIRDH	

Please turn over for details of how to enter ☞

H🌸w t🌸 enter

Listed overleaf are 15 jumbled-up names of flowers. All you have to do is unscramble the names and write your answer in the space provided. We've done the first one for you!

When you have found all the words, don't forget to fill in your name and address in the space provided below and pop this page into an envelope (you don't need a stamp) and post it today. Hurry—competition ends 31st August 1996.

Mills & Boon Flower Puzzle
FREEPOST
Croydon
Surrey
CR9 3WZ

Are you a Reader Service Subscriber?   Yes ❏   No ❏

Ms/Mrs/Miss/Mr _____

Address _____

_____

_____ Postcode _____

One application per household.

You may be mailed with other offers from other reputable companies as a result of this application. If you would prefer not to receive such offers, please tick box. ❏

COMP396
B